Artistic License to Kill
A FINE ART MYSTERY

Other Books by Paula Darnell

DIY Diva Mystery Series

Death by Association

Death by Design

Death by Proxy

Historical Mystery

The Six-Week Solution

Artistic License to Kill
A FINE ART MYSTERY

PAULA DARNELL

CR

Campbell and Rogers Press

Las Vegas

CR

Campbell and Rogers Press

Library of Congress Control Number: 2020906680
ISBN: 978-1-887402-12-5

Publisher's Cataloging-in-Publication Data
provided by Five Rainbows Cataloging Services

Names: Darnell, Paula, author.
Title: Artistic license to kill / Paula Darnell.
Description: Las Vegas : Campbell and Rogers Press, 2020. | Series: A fine art mystery, bk. 1.
Identifiers: LCCN 2020906680 (print) | ISBN 978-1-887402-12-5 (paperback) | ISBN 978-1-887402-13-2 (hardcover) | ISBN 978-1-887402-11-8 (ebook)
Subjects: LCSH: Murder—Fiction. | Artists—Fiction. | Art—Fiction. | Women—Fiction. | Arizona—Fiction. | Mystery fiction. | BISAC: FICTION / Mystery & Detective / Amateur Sleuth. | FICTION / Mystery & Detective / Cozy / Crafts. | FICTION / Mystery & Detective / Cozy / Cats & Dogs. | GSAFD: Mystery fiction.
Classification: LCC PS3604.A7478 A78 2020 (print) | LCC PS3604.A7478 (ebook) | DDC 813/.6—dc23.

Cover design by Nicole Hutton of Cover Shot Creations
Formatting by Polgarus Studio

First Edition

Published by Campbell and Rogers Press
www.campbellandrogerspress.com

*Dedicated, with love, to the memory of my parents,
Doris May Lindsey Darnell and James Roderick Darnell,
whose lifelong enjoyment of reading continues to inspire me*

Chapter 1

I squirmed in the hard metal chair as the three committee members examined the paintings I'd brought for their review.

The cordial, collegial chat I'd imagined when I'd applied to join the Roadrunner, a cooperative art gallery, had never happened. Instead, the director, a tall woman with cropped salt-and-pepper hair, had greeted me with a frown as I'd set up my canvases on the easels she'd provided.

The other two committee members—Travis Baxter, a wiry young man with long blond hair, and Pamela Smith, a tiny bird-like woman with sharp features—hadn't been any friendlier than the director. After glancing at my artist's statement and resumé, they'd peppered me with pointed questions that seemed framed to put me on the defensive. If that was their strategy, they'd succeeded.

As the three of them examined my paintings in silence, I clasped my hands firmly together so they wouldn't notice that I was trembling. Finally, the long-haired man cleared his throat and looked at the two women. They all returned to their seats behind a long table and looked at me solemnly.

Janice Warren, the gallery director, informed me that they'd take my application for membership under advisement and that

I'd be notified by mail as to whether or not I'd been approved to join the cooperative artists' group that ran the Roadrunner Gallery.

I managed to stammer a thank-you before I began gathering my canvases. I felt like running out of the gallery, but I restrained myself, knowing that I had to make two trips to my SUV to stow my paintings in the back.

The three committee members watched as I toted my canvases from the gallery's meeting room. Nobody offered to help me carry them. Nobody smiled at me.

As soon as I'd secured the last two paintings in my Toyota, I started the engine and peeled away from the curb. I couldn't wait to escape.

As I sped down Main Street, not bothering to glance in my rearview mirror, I heard the wail of a siren behind me. My tires screeched as I braked a little too hard.

A police car came alongside me, and the officer signaled me to pull over. Groaning, I slowly moved to the nearest parking space and stopped my SUV. It was still early in the morning, and the shops weren't open yet, so the street was nearly deserted.

While the police car parked in back of me, I reached into my purse and took out my Missouri driver's license; then I dug around inside the console next to me until I found my auto registration card. I put my window down and braced for a stern lecture.

"License and registration, please, ma'am."

I handed them to him. At least he'd said "please." Although I didn't much like being called "ma'am," since I would be reaching the big mid-century mark on my next birthday, I guessed it wouldn't be the last time it would happen.

"You must be in a big hurry to get back to Kansas City," he commented, staring at my license.

"Well, no. I'm sorry. I was upset, and I just wanted to put some distance between myself and the gallery."

"Oh?"

"I, uh, I applied to become a member, and I just had my interview there. It didn't go very well."

"You must live here now if you're joining the co-op."

I could have kicked myself for saying too much. Now, he'd probably cite me for not having an Arizona driver's license and not registering my SUV in my new state.

"Yes, I do. I moved here a few months ago." Again, too much information. I couldn't seem to stop babbling.

"If that's a permanent move, you should get your Arizona license and registration right away."

Great, I thought. *Could this day get any worse?* I wasn't looking forward to having more charges added to my speeding ticket.

"I'm not going to issue you a citation this time, but please watch your speed, ma'am. And don't forget to take care of your license and registration."

"I won't. I'll get it done right away. Thank you."

"Welcome to Arizona, ma'am," he said as he tipped his hat before returning to his cruiser.

Thankful to have at least dodged one bullet, I waited until his car was out of sight before driving slowly and cautiously home, where I knew I could count on a warm welcome from my golden retriever Laddie and tolerance, at least, from my calico cat Mona Lisa.

As I turned into my driveway, I saw my next-door neighbor, Belle, and her canine companion, Mr. Big, coming out of her house. By the time I parked in my carport and jumped out of my Toyota, Belle and Mr. Big were standing next to my driveway, waiting for me.

"Hi, Amanda," she said. "We were just on our way to the park. Would you and Laddie like to join us?"

Although I felt more like going into my hermit mode for the day than taking a walk with my neighbor, I realized that isolating myself wouldn't be very productive, and it certainly wouldn't make me feel any better about my botched interview.

"Sure," I agreed as I stooped to pet Mr. Big. Weighing in at a mere fifteen pounds, the energetic little white dog was, in fact, not so very big, and Laddie looked like a giant beside him. With his laid-back, sunny temperament, Laddie got along well with everyone, people and dogs alike, even cats, although they didn't always return the favor, and he and Mr. Big had become good pals in the two months since I'd moved to Lonesome Valley.

Assuring Belle that I wouldn't be a minute, I went inside, greeted my prancing dog, and quickly changed shoes as Mona Lisa watched us from atop her kitty tree. As soon as Laddie saw me grab his collar and leash, he ran to me and waited patiently while I snapped on his collar and attached his leash to it.

"That was quick," Belle said as we headed toward our neighborhood park, a short four-block walk away. "Are you feeling all right, Amanda? You look a little pale."

"Oh, do I? I'm not sick, but it's not even nine o'clock yet, and already it's been a stressful morning." As I told her about my disappointing interview and the traffic stop, Laddie and Mr. Big walked companionably in front of us, Mr. Big taking four steps for every one of Laddie's.

"Amanda, that's terrible!" Belle exclaimed. "I've always thought the Roadrunner was such a nice gallery, and the artists are always friendly and helpful whenever I pop in. I buy a lot of artists' greeting cards there."

I nodded. "That's what I thought, too, the very first time I went into the gallery. In fact, it was one of the reasons I moved here. I never imagined they might turn me down, and I was counting on some sales from the Roadrunner to bolster my income. With my budget as tight as it is, I guess I'll have to come up with a Plan B soon."

"Don't give up hope yet," my neighbor advised me. "They haven't actually turned you down. Who knows? They may accept your application."

"Hmm, like that's going to happen," I said glumly. I knew Belle was trying to cheer me up, but I didn't feel very cheerful. I mentally kicked myself for counting on the Roadrunner as another venue to sell my paintings before my membership had been approved.

Belle gently squeezed my arm, and a look of sympathy crossed her face. "I know it can be tough, moving and getting established in a new place. When Dennis and I moved here ten years ago, we thought we could retire early and never have to work again, but we miscalculated. We were lucky, though, because Dennis was so bored with retirement that he wanted to go back to work, anyway." Belle's husband Dennis managed a local feed store. I'd assumed he'd been there for decades.

"You make a good point," I said. "Our plans don't always work out the way we hope. I'll figure something out." I was afraid that Plan B might mean getting a job, instead of earning my living as a full-time artist. The one thing I knew about having a boss and working for someone else all day was that it spoiled everything.

Chapter 2

I didn't share that thought with Belle, but as we continued our walk, circling the park. I remembered how little time I'd had to paint during all the years I'd worked full-time in my ex-husband's insurance agency.

"Maybe I could get a part-time job," I mused aloud.

"Dennis can always use another clerk at the feed store," Belle said, "if it comes to that. All you need to do is say the word, but don't you think you should wait to hear from the Roadrunner?"

"I guess so, but I can't imagine they'll invite me to join. Not one committee member so much as cracked a shadow of a smile the whole time I was there."

Belle and I were so engrossed in our conversation that we didn't hear a runner coming up behind us. At about the same time, Mr. Big spotted a pair of terriers on the other side of the park, and he ran toward them, jerking his leash from Belle's hand. Leaving the path, she started to run after Mr. Big when the jogger collided with her, and they both went down hard.

"Ouch!" Belle exclaimed as the jogger, a teenage girl, bounced back up as though she had springs on her feet, muttered "sorry," and took off running.

"Hey!" I shouted after her, but she kept on running without a backward glance.

In the meantime, Mr. Big had approached the terriers, and the three dogs were engaged in a barking contest.

"Are you OK?" I asked, kneeling next to Belle, who was rubbing her right ankle and hadn't made a move to stand up.

"I'm not sure. My ankle really hurts. I guess I should try to stand up and see if I can put any weight on it."

Belle attempted to get up, but her ankle wasn't cooperating, and I feared she might have broken it.

"I guess that's a 'no,'" she said ruefully, as the owner of the terriers came over to us, with Mr. Big and his own dogs in tow.

"I saw what happened," the dog walker, a husky bald man of about sixty, said. "It's hard to believe that young girl didn't stop to help. I'm Greg Winters, by the way." He nodded toward the houses on the other side of the street. "I live right over there. May I offer you ladies a ride home?"

After we'd introduced ourselves and our dogs, Greg and I helped Belle to her feet. Leaning on us, she hopped to a nearby park bench, and I sat beside her, keeping a firm grip on Mr. Big's leash, while Greg took his terriers home. He returned, along with his wife Rebecca, and parked his car on the street near the bench.

After we supported Belle while she hopped over to the car, Belle and I squeezed into the back seat. Laddie sandwiched himself between Belle and me, and Mr. Big curled up on Belle's lap for the short ride home.

I looked at her ankle, and I could see that it had swollen considerably. Rebecca must have noticed it, too, because she suggested that we go directly to the emergency room at our local hospital.

"But I don't have my license and insurance card or even my cell phone with me," Belle protested. "I need to go home and get them. Anyway, I think my own doctor can probably see me, so I shouldn't have to go to the hospital. I'll call her office as soon as we get home."

"I can take you to your doctor's office," I volunteered. "And I'm afraid we'd better pick up some crutches for you, too."

Belle sighed. "You're right. I have a feeling I'm going to need them for a while."

As we'd feared, Belle's doctor confirmed that she'd sprained her ankle and predicted it would take several weeks for a full recovery. She instructed Belle to ice her ankle, elevate it, wear a compression bandage, and stay off her feet as much as possible for the next two days. She recommended over-the-counter pain relievers, too. After we left the doctor's office, we drove to the drug store, and Belle waited in the car while I went in and rented a pair of aluminum crutches and purchased a compression bandage. Belle said she had an ice pack and ibuprofen at home.

"Thanks, Amanda," Belle said. "I really appreciate your help."

"No problem. Let's get you home where you can put your feet up."

By this time, it was noon. Since I'd been too nervous before my interview to eat breakfast, I felt hungry, so I suggested picking up some fast food or ordering a pizza. Belle opted for a pizza. After we decided on a large veggie supreme, she called in our order for delivery while I drove back to her house.

"Half an hour," she said as she put her cell phone in her purse. "I hope I can maneuver with those crutches."

"You'll get the hang of it. I twisted my ankle once when I was in college, and I had to use crutches for a week or so. By the way, have you called Dennis yet?"

"Yes, and he wanted to rush home, but I told him I'll be hanging out on the couch for the afternoon, and there's really no need. I think I convinced him that he might as well stay at work until the store closes."

"Home at last," I said as I parked in her driveway.

"Well, here goes nothing," Belle said.

I helped her out of the car, and handed her the crutches. She steadied herself as she gripped the crutches and swung forward with a little hop.

"You're doing fine," I assured her as she slowly made her way to the house, only a few yards away.

Mr. Big greeted us at the door. The wiggling little dog ran around in circles, and I was afraid Belle might trip over her excited canine, so I picked him up and cuddled him in my arms while she settled herself on the sofa, placing the crutches on the side of the couch so that she could reach them.

She held her arms out for Mr. Big, and he happily curled up on her lap while she petted him. I propped a pillow under her ankle, put the ice pack in the freezer, and handed her a bottle of water along with an ibuprofen tablet.

"Thanks, Amanda," she said, popping the pill into her mouth and taking a few sips of water. When she was done, she flashed me a weak grin. "I'll be glad when my ankle stops throbbing."

"The ice pack should help," I told her. "It'll be cold enough soon. Would you like a soft drink with your pizza?"

"No, thanks. I'll stick to water," she said, raising the bottle. "But help yourself to whatever you'd like. I have cold iced tea, soft drinks, and plenty of water in the fridge. When the pizza comes, could you please give Mr. Big a chewy? That'll keep him distracted while we eat. They're in the pantry on the bottom shelf."

"Sure, and I'll grab some plates and napkins for us, too."

I was on my way back to the kitchen when the doorbell rang. Mr. Big jumped down and, barking, ran to the door. I didn't want him to run outside when I opened the door, so I picked him up again and cradled him in one arm while I opened the door.

I nearly fainted when I saw the delivery man. He was none other than the young guy with long hair who'd interviewed me that very morning. His long blond hair was pulled back in a pony tail, and he wore a baseball cap pulled low over his forehead, but he was the same man, all right.

"Large veggie supreme," he announced, unzipping the insulated sleeve surrounding the pizza. He lifted the lid of the box so that I could see the pizza.

I was still taken aback. When I didn't say anything, he looked up and his expression said it all: he felt as awkward as I did.

"It's Mrs. Trent, isn't it?"

"Ms. Trent, actually. Amanda." I recovered myself enough to ask him to come in and put the pizza on the coffee table. Mr. Big had spotted a cat on the other side of the street, and he was far too interested in the feline for me to let him down while the door was open.

"And I'm Chip," he said, placing the pizza box on the coffee table.

Chip? He'd been introduced to me as Travis at the gallery. I supposed Chip must be his nickname.

Belle handed him cash and told him to keep the change. He thanked her and headed for the door. As he was about to make his exit, he turned and looked at me.

"You're a wonderful artist," he said with a wink, and then he was gone.

Chapter 3

The letter from the Roadrunner Gallery came the very next day. In a warm tone, it welcomed me to the artists' cooperative group that ran the gallery. According to the letter, I'd been assigned a mentor, an experienced gallery member who would show me the ropes. Members were required to work in the gallery two days each month, except for the first month when we had to put in five days, accompanied by our assigned mentor. The letter was signed "Cordially" by the stern gallery director, Janice Warren, and she'd included a handwritten postscript at the bottom: "Welcome to the Roadrunner!"

I gave a little whoop of joy, which immediately roused Laddie and Mona Lisa from their afternoon naps. Laddie ran to me, and Mona Lisa came over and wound herself around my ankles. I leaned over and petted them both. I could always count on Laddie, who never strayed far from my side, but Mona Lisa was a bit fickle. At times, she loved to settle herself in my lap or lie next to me while I slept; other times, she took to her perch, surveying Laddie and me from on high.

I called Belle right away to tell her the good news.

"That's great, Amanda!" she enthused. "I'm glad they let

you know so soon. Now you don't have to worry they'll turn you down."

"I was sure they would," I agreed, "but then when Chip winked at me, I began to wonder. I still wonder why they acted the way they did during my interview, but I guess it doesn't matter much now."

"You're in. That's the important thing."

"Yes. And now, enough about me! How are you doing? Do you need anything?"

At lunchtime earlier, I'd taken Belle a casserole and some oatmeal cookies I'd made. She hadn't been having any trouble getting around the house with her crutches, but she'd been bored with having to keep her ankle elevated, which considerably limited what she could do.

"No, thanks, Amanda. I'm getting along all right—about as well as I can, I suppose. Right now, I'm trying to decide whether to take a nap or watch that new thriller on Netflix. Dennis is going to make us dinner tonight, so I'm all set."

"Well, OK, but be sure to let me know if you need anything."

After I talked to Belle, I re-read my letter of acceptance. My mentor's name was Susan Carpenter. Both her phone number and her email address were listed in the letter. Since I was eager to get started, I decided to give her a call, but my call went to voice mail. Disappointed, I left a message introducing myself and telling Susan the reason for my call.

Laddie followed me into my studio, where I put a few finishing touches on a commissioned landscape. I was pleased with the large piece, but worried about shipping it back to Kansas City. The buyers, a prominent judge and his wife, an equally prominent city official, had commissioned the artwork after attending the opening of my one-and-only solo show at a small gallery in Kansas City.

I'll never forget that June evening. My daughter Emma, on her summer break after her first year at a small, private college in California, and my son Dustin, a corporate accountant who'd been recently promoted at his firm, were there, along with my parents, who'd flown in from Florida, especially for the occasion. The gallery owner, Crystal Star, couldn't have been more enthusiastic as she circulated around the gallery, introducing the attendees to my work. Champagne flowed, and a pleasant, positive buzz rose in the room as Crystal placed signs proclaiming "SOLD" under three of my paintings.

I'd felt mildly irritated that Ned, my husband, had arrived late. His tardiness had become a habit during the previous couple months, but I didn't want to spoil the opening by complaining about it, so I didn't say anything. By this time, the judge and his wife had already approached me about painting a landscape for them, and I was over the moon.

After the show, my parents insisted on taking us all out to dinner, and we didn't get home until around midnight.

That's when Ned dropped the bomb.

He told me he was getting a divorce, handed me a sheaf of official documents, and told me to sign them. Then he walked out. I was so stunned that I couldn't speak.

My ringing phone brought me back to the present. Susan Carpenter was returning my call.

"It's been a while since we had a new member at the Roadrunner. I can't wait to see your paintings, Amanda. We probably should get together as soon as possible because you'll be able to hang your paintings in the gallery this Saturday night," Susan said. "Most of our artists change their displays.

on the first Saturday of the month."

"That's great! I didn't realize I'd be able to hang my work so soon. If you're not busy, I could meet you in a few minutes."

"As a matter of fact, that works for me. Would you mind if I came over to your place? I'd love to see your paintings."

I told Susan that would be fine and gave her my address. While I waited for her arrival, I tidied my studio, arranging some of the paintings I planned to hang at the Roadrunner on easels around the room. I didn't move the judge's landscape since the paint was still wet. Oil paint could take forever to dry, but I was learning that the low Arizona humidity helped out a bit on that score.

The doorbell rang, just as I finished. Laddie ran to the door, his feathery tale sweeping back and forth as he awaited our visitor. When I opened the door, he stood politely beside me while I invited Susan to come inside.

"A golden!" she exclaimed, as she petted my friendly retriever.

"This is Laddie," I said, as my dog soaked up attention from his latest admirer. Susan was short, about my height, and her brown hair fell in soft waves to her shoulders. I guessed she was probably a few years younger than me. She was dressed casually in jeans and a drapey tunic, and she carried a large brown envelope.

She held up the envelope. "Paperwork from the gallery. It's pretty standard stuff—our policies and procedures, the gallery schedule, inventory sheets and tags. The usual," she said as she handed it to me. "I highlighted all the places you need to sign with a yellow marker."

"Thanks. I'll be sure to take care of it today." I set the bulging envelope on an end table. "Shall we go into the studio? It's right through here." I opened the door to my six-hundred-square-foot studio. It was actually the same size as the rest of the house, which was divided into a living room, a kitchen, one bedroom, and one bathroom.

"What a wonderful space!" Susan enthused.

"Yes. I was lucky to find it. It was the only house with a studio available for rent in Lonesome Valley when I moved here."

"I think you're going to do very well at the Roadrunner," Susan told me. "Your paintings are every bit as good as Chip said they are."

"Thank you. That's nice to hear."

"Chip's my nephew," Susan added. "He wants to be a full-time artist, but it isn't easy. He's been out of college a few years, but he still lives at home and works at my brother's pizzeria."

No wonder my art judge was doubling as a pizza delivery man. His father owned the pizza parlor.

If I didn't start selling some of my artwork locally, I might be delivering pizzas soon, too. Either that or clerking at the feed store.

Since neither alternative appealed much to me, I resolved to re-double my efforts and stick to Plan A for as long as my money lasted.

Chapter 4

The Roadrunner closed at five o'clock on Saturdays. As soon as all the customers departed, the artists could begin changing their displays. Susan told me that, although it wasn't mandatory to change the artwork every month, many members did just that. Gallery artists were each allotted fifteen linear feet of wall space, and they could arrange their paintings or other two-dimensional artwork as they chose, as long as they stayed within the confines of their own space. Sculptors, ceramists, and jewelry artists were assigned pedestals or cases for their three-dimensional works.

Susan had volunteered to pick me up and guide me through the check-in process. Together we'd selected which paintings I'd be displaying and discussed how to arrange them for the best effect.

We arrived at the gallery shortly after five, and Susan introduced me to several artists as we made our way through the gallery to a table where Janice Warren, the gallery director, was checking in the artwork. She hadn't been in the gallery that morning when I'd stopped by to drop off my signed paperwork, my check for the yearly membership fee, and my first month's rent. As I handed over my check, I felt a brief moment of panic, knowing how puny the balance in my bank account would look after the gallery cashed the check, but I reminded myself that I could always fall back to Plan B, if necessary.

"Hello, Susan," Janice greeted my mentor. "Ah, and here's our new member. Glad to have you with us, Amanda."

Although Janice's words were welcoming, her demeanor was as stern as it had been during my interview.

"Thank you," I said. "I'm thrilled to be here."

Slight crinkles appeared at the corners of Janice's mouth. I guessed that was her version of a smile. She quickly checked that the numbers on my paintings matched those on my inventory sheet and tags and handed me a floor plan, indicating where I could find my wall space. Susan and I went to work hanging my paintings. We arranged them and re-arranged them until we were satisfied with the display. Susan stepped back and gazed at my wall.

"Amanda, you do great work. I'd be willing to bet you'll sell a couple paintings this month."

"I really hope so."

"I know so," a masculine voice added. I turned to see Chip, who grinned at me.

"It can't hurt to be optimistic, I suppose," I said.

Chip nodded and winked at me.

"I snagged a parking spot right in front of the gallery, Aunt Susan," Chip said.

"Oh, good. I'll be right with you. Back in a few minutes, Amanda. I need to help Chip unload his truck."

"I can help, too," I offered.

"No need. We have it covered. Stay here and meet some of the other members. I know they'll want to talk to you."

After Susan left, I noticed that one of my smaller paintings looked slightly askew. I was gently nudging it back into place when Janice came over.

"Do you mind if I make a suggestion?" she asked.

Instantly, I froze. I know Janice must have noticed my deer-in-the-headlights expression, but she plunged ahead without waiting for my reply.

"I've been the gallery director here for twenty years, and I know what sells. I strongly advise you to frame your paintings, with the proper framing, of course. I can recommend an excellent framer in Scottsdale, who does high-quality work."

"Well, I don't know," I hedged. "I've always shown gallery-wrap paintings. That way, buyers can have them framed to suit their own taste or hang them just the way they are."

"Of course, that's true, but I think it's up to the artist to present a complete and cohesive piece. You can accomplish that with the right framing and make your paintings more salable at the same time."

The last thing I wanted to do was argue with the gallery director on my first evening as a member, but the fact was I simply couldn't afford to pay for framing, which didn't come cheap, especially if it was high quality.

I could feel a warm blush coming on. I'm sure my face was beet red by the time I answered Janice.

"I'm afraid I can't afford to have any of my paintings framed right now," I confessed. "I'm on a very tight budget. Maybe sometime in the future . . . ," I trailed off, giving Janice the opportunity to pounce again.

"But surely you could buy frames on credit. I know Marcel's in Scottsdale takes any major credit card."

Did she really believe that I didn't know that frame shops took credit cards? Mine just happened to be very close to its limit. I could feel little beads of perspiration popping out on my face.

A commotion near the front of the gallery sidetracked our conversation. I heard cries of "wow!" and "look at that!" Then a "bravo, Susan!" People crowded near the gallery entrance. Above them, I could see the head and long spotted neck of a large giraffe.

Janice and I both joined the crowd. When we moved closer, I could see the smooth, lustrous finish on the tall animal. Surely it couldn't be ceramic, I thought.

"Where would you like me to put her?" Susan asked Janice.

"Right in front of the window," Janice replied. "Over here." She pointed. "I marked your floor space with masking tape."

When Chip lifted the creature with ease, I figured it was made of papier-mâché. He placed it on the spot Janice had indicated. Susan rotated it a few inches at a time until the gallery director was satisfied with its position. The big giraffe was at least two feet taller than I am. I looked up at its benevolent face, admiring the clever way Susan had painted it. My mentor had told me about her floral watercolors, but she'd neglected to mention that she sculpted, too.

"Susan, what a surprise! You didn't tell me that you're a sculptor."

She smiled an enigmatic smile that reminded me of why I'd named my cat Mona Lisa.

"I wanted to see your reaction when I brought Lola in."

"You named your giraffe Lola?"

"She seems like a Lola."

"I guess she does, at that, with her fabulous long, curly eyelashes." I gently stroked Lola's side. "How did you ever manage to get such a smooth surface on her?"

"It's taken me a decade of experimenting to finally settle on the techniques that work best. The short version is that there are several layers of paper clay of different consistencies and then, of course, coats of varnish after I do the painting. I also sand the surface before I paint it."

"Well, she's just wonderful."

I backed up as other artists crowded around Susan to discuss Lola. Finally, the hubbub died down, most of the artists drifted back to their own displays, and Janice returned to the table in the back. A few members followed her, and she handed them each a sheet of paper.

"Am I missing something?" I asked Susan. "It looks like Janice is handing out some kind of paperwork."

"No worries. It's just the monthly schedule for working in the gallery. When I talked to Janice yesterday, she promised she'd schedule us together for the days we requested."

"Would you mind picking up a copy of the schedule for me, too? I don't want to talk to Janice again right at the moment."

"Uh, oh. What happened?"

Since I'd already confided in Susan about my precarious financial status two days earlier when she first visited me, I didn't mind telling her about my latest embarrassment.

"Janice is like a bulldog when she gets an idea in her head. Don't be surprised if she brings it up again. At least, next time you'll be prepared."

"I'm not so sure about that!"

"We can head out now if you'd rather not talk to her again this evening."

"You don't mind?"

"Not at all."

"Wait. What about the schedule? Shouldn't we check it to

verify that we work the days we wanted?"

"No problem. Janice always posts it online right after everyone's finished with their set-ups. Shall we go to Miguel's for dinner? They make the best enchiladas in town, and, more important, they make a mean margarita. My treat."

"Sounds good," I agreed. "I'd love a margarita right about now.

Chapter 5

As Susan had predicted, the Roadrunner's online schedule had confirmed that we would be able to work at the gallery on the days we'd requested.

On Tuesday, our first day together at the gallery, I met Susan a few minutes before nine o'clock, in front of the gallery. She explained that, since Janice lived in the apartment above the Roadrunner and made it a point to stay in the building during the hours the gallery was open, she admitted members who showed up to work in the morning, and she always closed the gallery herself.

"I happen to have a key, too," Susan said, "because I used to be a board member, but I've never had to use it. Janice always opens the door for me." She pulled her cell phone from her jacket pocket and poked it. "That's odd. She's not answering."

"Maybe she stepped out to run an errand."

"That's really not like her. I'll try again." Janice didn't answer the second phone call, either. "Well, this is a first. I guess I'll have to use my key, after all." She dug deep inside her purse and produced a ring of keys. "I remember marking it with red nail polish. Ah, here it is."

Susan inserted the key into the front door lock and struggled with it briefly. She jiggled it a bit more, and the lock finally cooperated.

I followed her inside. Susan stepped to the left and turned on the overhead lights. I looked toward the back of the gallery. Although a divider wall obscured part of the rear area, I could see that something was amiss. A bronze sculpture of a bear lay on the floor. It had been the only bronze in the back room when I'd arranged my paintings for display on Saturday evening.

I walked to the back, picked up the small statue, and restored it to its place atop a wooden pedestal.

"What in the world?" Susan said from her vantage point behind me.

We both looked around the room, but nothing else appeared to be out of place.

"I wonder how that happened," I said.

Susan frowned. "Janice isn't going to be happy when we tell her we found her bear on the floor."

"I didn't realize she was a sculptor."

"Yes, I know she takes a dim view of my papier-mâché animals, but since they always sell, she hasn't complained to me lately."

"But she has to someone else?" I guessed.

Susan nodded. "She told Pamela that they didn't belong in the same gallery with her bronzes. She said you can't really call yourself a sculptor unless you work in stone or have your art pieces cast in metal."

"I'd have to disagree with her."

"Me, too!" Susan said vehemently. "Well, I guess we'd better set up. Customers could show up any minute. We need to sign in and get the cash for the register from the office. I'll show you where we keep everything."

Just off the main gallery a hallway led to a classroom that doubled as a meeting room for the members, the same room where I'd had my interview a week earlier. An office, restroom, kitchenette, and supply closet were on the right side of the hallway, and the large classroom was on the left. My knowledge of the layout came from a floor plan that had been included in my membership packet. The day I'd had my interview, I hadn't had the time or inclination to explore the members' area of the gallery.

We rounded the corner to the little alcove where the arched entry to the hallway was.

That's when we saw her—her feet, that is.

Janice was lying face down in the hallway, her feet extending into the alcove. Her head was at an odd angle, and her hair was matted with blood. A little puddle of it had dripped onto the hardwood floor beneath her.

"Oh, no!" Susan shrieked. For a moment, I thought she'd turn and run, but she hurried to Janice's side and knelt next to her, She grabbed Janice's wrist, than dropped it and pressed her fingers to Janice's neck.

In the meantime, I speed dialed 9-1-1 to call for help.

"What's your emergency?" the operator asked calmly.

"Please send an ambulance. A woman has been seriously injured." I explained that we'd just come into the gallery and found Janice lying on the floor with a head wound.

Susan looked at me and shook her head.

"We think she may be dead," I added.

Susan stood up and motioned for me to give her the phone. In a daze, I listened as she told the dispatcher that Janice wasn't breathing and had no pulse.

Just a moment later, we heard a siren, and we went to the

front of the gallery and saw a police car, lights flashing, pulling up to the curb. A brief whoop sounded as the siren stopped abruptly.

I recognized the young officer as the same man who'd stopped me for speeding right after my interview. When he saw me, I could tell that he recognized me, too, but neither of us said anything about our previous encounter. We quickly led him to Janice, and he performed some of the same maneuvers that Susan had used before he stood and asked us to wait for him in the front of the gallery. We could hear him calling in a report, requesting back-up.

Within minutes, the place swarmed with police, and a coroner's van had parked in back of the young officer's patrol car. The ambulance that had been dispatched was sent on its way, and we were told to wait outside the gallery for Lieutenant Belmont, the detective who'd been assigned to investigate. There were wooden benches on the sidewalks up and down Main Street, courtesy of the Lonesome Valley Downtown Merchants' Association, so we sat, stunned, on the bench outside the Roadrunner while we waited for the lieutenant.

Susan dabbed her eyes with a tissue.

"I didn't always see eye to eye with Janice. In fact, I'll even admit she was one of my least favorite people, but no one deserves being bashed over the head the way she was."

"It's truly awful," I agreed My hand trembled as I gently touched her arm. Although I'd met Janice only twice and had found her somewhat intimidating, the horror of her untimely death would stay with me forever.

With the arrival of the police and ambulance, a crowd of spectators had gathered, but since the area in front of the gallery had been cordoned off, they weren't near us.

"I need to call Pamela and Tiffany to let them know what happened. They're scheduled to work from one to five this afternoon."

Susan fumbled for her cell phone and was about to make a call when the young officer who had first responded to our emergency call came over.

"Ma'am," he began, but this time he was addressing Susan. I wondered whether he called all women of a certain age "ma'am." "Please don't contact anyone until after you've spoken to Lieutenant Belmont."

"But I need to alert the members who are supposed to work in the gallery this afternoon not to come in today. I assume we're closed for the day, aren't we?"

"Yes. Probably longer, but you'll have to speak with the lieutenant about that."

Just then my own cell phone rang. When I saw that Belle was calling, I automatically started to answer.

"Please don't answer that," the young cop said.

"But . . . ," I protested, reluctantly returning my phone to my pocket.

"Look, ladies, I'm sure the lieutenant will be here soon. While you're waiting, I'm going to go next door and get you coffee. You both look as though you could use some. Any preferences—latte, mocha?"

"I'll have a latte with soy milk. Thank you, officer," Susan said.

I opted for a mocha minus the whipped cream. He returned a few minutes later and handed us the steaming brew.

"Thank you," I said, accepting the drink. "Let me pay you for these." I grabbed my purse. I figured a small town patrol officer probably had to struggle just like I did to make ends meet.

"It's on the house. The Coffee Klatsch always gives anyone on the force a freebie. The brass told us not to take too much advantage, though."

"Mike, front and center," one of the other officers called. "Belmont's here." He pointed to a portly man wearing a rumpled jacket. I guessed he was probably my age or maybe a little older. The young policeman and Lieutenant Belmont disappeared into the gallery, but it wasn't long before both emerged, and the detective motioned for us to join him.

"I understand you gals found the body."

Gals? Where had he been for the last hundred years?

"Yes," Susan answered.

"Tell me what happened," he said to Susan. "And don't you interrupt," he said to me. "I'll get to you later."

Susan obliged him while I seethed at his rude manner.

"Anything else you can think of?" This question was directed at me, rather than Susan, so I added that I'd found the bronze bear on the floor when we arrived and that I'd put it back on its pedestal.

"Why didn't *you* tell me about that?" he snapped at Susan, who immediately burst into tears.

"I forgot," she stammered between sobs.

My turn was next.

"Why did you touch the evidence?" he demanded.

"I had no way of knowing the bear was evidence. We hadn't found Janice yet at that point."

He didn't look particularly mollified by my explanation, and he directed me to go to the police station immediately to have my fingerprints taken.

"Dyson, get over here!" the lieutenant bellowed, motioning impatiently to the officer who'd brought us coffee.

"Make sure Dyson has your contact information," he told us before stalking off. Officer Dyson had been lingering close by, and he'd evidently heard everything Lieutenant Belmont had said to us.

"Sorry about that," the young cop said sheepishly. "He's not the most diplomatic person on the force."

Susan was still dabbing her eyes as we handed over our licenses, and he took a picture of them with his cell phone.

"New license I see, Mrs. Trent."

I didn't feel up to telling him I wasn't a Mrs. anymore.

"Yes, I'm officially an Arizonan now, I guess." I was glad I'd followed through on my promise to him to change my license and auto registration to my new state.

He nodded. "Well, I guess that's it, except for your phone numbers. See Sergeant Martinez at the station for your fingerprints." He held up his phone. "I'll give him a heads-up, so he'll be expecting you."

We thanked him and threaded our way through the crowd that was still milling around, outside the barriers the police had set up.

Once we reached Susan's car, we sat there for a few minutes, sipping our coffee.

"I just can't believe Janice is dead—murdered!" Susan wailed. When she'd calmed down a little, she said, "I'd better call Pamela and Tiffany first, since they were scheduled to work this afternoon. I can ask Pamela to let the other members know."

"And I should give my neighbor a call. She's probably wondering why I didn't pick up when she called a few minutes ago."

Before either of us had the chance to make our calls, my

phone rang. I answered immediately when I saw it was Belle.

"Thank goodness! I was so worried about you. Dennis went into work late today, and he called to tell me he saw a bunch of police cars and the coroner's van parked right outside the gallery. He didn't realize you were going to be working there this morning, or he would have stopped to make sure you were all right."

"We found Janice, the gallery director, lying on the floor, but it was too late. There was nothing we could do for her."

"How terrible! I suppose she must have had a heart attack or a stroke."

"I'm afraid not. She was murdered."

Chapter 6

"Murder *here* in Lonesome Valley? I can't believe it! You're lucky you didn't get there earlier. The killer might have still been lurking around the gallery."

"You're right," I said with a shudder. That scary thought hadn't even occurred to me yet, but if Belle hadn't brought it up, I probably would have thought of it myself eventually.

"Are you on your way home now?"

"After a stop at the police station." I explained about the fingerprints.

"Why don't you come over when you get home and bring Laddie with you. He can play with Mr. Big while we have lunch."

"I don't want you to go to any trouble. You still need to take it easy."

"It's no trouble. I'm managing fairly well with my crutches. Dennis made us a nice artichoke-potato frittata for breakfast. We can have the rest of it for lunch. I'll make a salad."

"Well, all right, if you're sure."

"I'm sure. You shouldn't be alone at a time like this."

Fortunately, the fingerprinting didn't take long, thanks to Sergeant Martinez's efficiency, and I was soon sitting at the picnic table on Belle's patio with a plate of artichoke-potato frittata and salad in front of me while Laddie and Mr. Big romped in the backyard.

Of course, I had to tell Belle all about what happened from the moment Susan and I had arrived at the gallery. Belle listened without interrupting.

"I guess I still feel shaky," I admitted when I'd finished my narrative.

"No wonder. Lonesome Valley's hardly a crime center. We've lived here for ten years, and I can't remember there ever being a murder in town. It's just terrible. And in a shop right on Main Street. Whoever did it must be quite bold. I wonder why someone would want to kill the director of the Roadrunner. Do you think it could have been a robbery?"

"I don't think so. Susan told me that they make a bank deposit at the end of each day, and they keep just enough cash on hand to make change the following morning. Except for the bronze bear, none of the artwork had been disturbed. I don't know about Janice's apartment upstairs, though. It's possible she may have had some valuable jewelry there or maybe even cash, but I really have no idea."

I felt restless and unsettled after the terrible events of the morning, so when we finished lunch, I volunteered to take the dogs for a walk. I knew there was no way I'd be able to do any painting today, as distracted as I felt.

As soon as Laddie and Mr. Big saw me grab their leashes, they came running, eager for their next adventure.

Belle waved as we departed, saying she was going to take a power nap while we were gone. Since the dogs had expended a considerable amount of energy playing already, they didn't strain at their leashes. Laddie kept pace with me nicely, while Mr. Big made sure that Laddie never put a step ahead of him.

Soon, we arrived at the park. Although Laddie and I had taken walks in the last few days, this was the first time we'd come back to the park since Belle's unfortunate accident. I felt a twinge of nostalgia as we passed the playground where a couple of young mothers were supervising their toddlers. Those days were gone for me.

Now, here I was in a new town with none of my family living nearby. I didn't really feel lonely, but I was keenly aware that, except for Laddie and Mona Lisa, I was alone. Janice had died alone. I couldn't get the image of her lying dead in the hallway at the gallery out of my head, and I knew that image would stay with me forever.

Suddenly, Laddie yelped and held up his right front paw. "Sit, Laddie," I told him, and he complied. I tried to get Mr. Big to do the same, but he didn't cooperate. He wiggled so much that it was difficult to control him and examine Laddie's paw at the same time. I sat on the grass next to the sidewalk and plunked Mr. Big in my lap.

"Let's see your paw, boy," I said, reaching for it. Laddie seemed to understand, and he didn't move while I gingerly raised his paw. I could see the cause of his distress immediately. There was a thin, spiky thorn in the pad of his foot. Luckily, it wasn't embedded too deeply, and I was able to yank it out.

"It's OK now, Laddie," I assured him. He jumped up and pranced around me, seemingly no worse for wear. Mr. Big jumped out of my lap to join him and began emitting joyful little yelps. I heard other dogs barking, too, and when I turned to see where the racket was coming from, I spotted Rebecca and Greg Winter approaching us with their two terriers.

"We meet again," Greg said. "Everything OK? We saw you sitting on the ground."

"It is now. Laddie had a thorn in his paw, but I pulled it out, and he seems fine now."

"How's your friend getting along?" Rebecca asked. "Is her ankle broken?"

"Not broken, but she has a bad sprain. Her doctor said a full recovery will take several weeks. She's managing with crutches."

"You know we saw that same jogger who knocked her down again. She came awfully close to ramming into a baby stroller yesterday. I wish I knew where she lived. Her parents need to take her in hand. That girl is a menace," Greg declared.

I had to agree with him. If the careless teenager had been paying attention, she could have easily avoided running into Belle.

After a frenzy of sniffing and scrambling around each other, the dogs settled down. Laddie rolled in the grass while the terriers and Mr. Big stood next to each other, wagging their tails.

"Just look at them. Not a care in the world," Rebecca said, smiling at the cute canines.

"I wish I could say the same."

"What is it, Amanda? Is something wrong?"

"There's been a murder here in town, and I discovered the victim," I blurted out. "I joined the Roadrunner Gallery a few days ago, and when I went there to work this morning, there she was."

"That's terrible! A murder in Lonesome Valley! I've always thought our community was safe. Say, you weren't all alone, were you?" Greg asked.

"No, I was with another member. The woman who was killed was the gallery director."

"Not Janice Trent," Rebecca said.

"Yes, it was Janice. Do you know her?"

"I sure do . . . er, did. We went to high school together here in Lonesome Valley. Her sister used to be a good friend of mine. She moved to Texas after high school, but whenever she came back to town to visit Janice, she'd call me and we'd get together. Somewhere along the line, we lost touch, though. I haven't seen Judith for about seven or eight years now, ever since she had a big blow-up with Janice. They stopped speaking, and Judith stopped visiting. I wonder if she'll come back here for the funeral. I always regretted losing track of her. Of course, that was my fault as much as hers."

"I think we should get going, honey," Greg told his wife. "I need to alert the neighborhood watch members. We don't want to be snoozing while a murderer's on the loose. Amanda, you should be extra careful, too. Make sure you're never alone in that gallery, and lock all your doors and windows at home."

I didn't really think I was in danger, but I certainly couldn't blame Greg for his caution. I assured him that I'd take care before we went our separate ways. On our walk home from the park, I thought about the murder, and it seemed to me that the killer either must have targeted Janice deliberately or argued with her and struck her a heavy blow in anger. Most likely, either Janice had admitted the assailant to the gallery herself, or a key holder had unlocked the door and come in without Janice's knowledge. As much as I hated to believe it, I thought it likely that the killer was a member of the gallery cooperative. Susan had already told Pamela and Tiffany that she and I were the ones who'd discovered Janice's body, so soon all the members would know. Even so, unless we had actually seen the killer, he or she had no reason to come after Susan or me.

Despite my rationalizations, I would definitely be locking all the doors and windows in my house and the studio from now on.

Chapter 7

We didn't linger at Belle's after dropping off Mr. Big. Mona Lisa was waiting for us at home, and as soon as I removed Laddie's leash, she began meowing piteously. I picked her up and cradled her in my arms, and she began to purr. I never knew how Mona Lisa would react to my absence. Sometimes she wanted nothing to do with me after I returned, and the length of time I left her didn't seem to make much difference, nor did Laddie's presence or lack thereof.

"Are you feeling neglected, Mona Lisa?" I asked, and she responded with an ear-splitting meow.

To pacify her, I grabbed one of her feather toys and began playing with her while Laddie watched us but didn't try to join the game. Every time I flicked the feather, Mona Lisa pounced, and, then, teasing, I would quickly move it again. She never tired of this game, although I couldn't say the same.

"Enough for now," I said after we'd played for several minutes. To distract her, I gave her a tuna kitty treat. She loved tuna and quickly dispatched it before leaping to the top of her kitty perch and looking down on Laddie and me. Naturally, Laddie had to have a treat, too, so I spooned a few chunks of leftover tuna into his bowl.

With the pets temporarily placated, I wandered into my studio. Laddie trailed behind me and settled himself on his bed in the corner, where he could keep a watchful eye on me. Whenever I made a move to leave the studio, whether to step into our cozy little abode or to go out the back door into the yard, Laddie would jump up and follow me.

While he curled up for a siesta, I picked up my digital camera and took some photos of the landscape I'd just completed for the judge and his wife. I'd told them it would be completed by the end of April and that I would ship it to them at no charge because they'd commissioned the painting when I still lived in Kansas City. When we'd signed the contract, I had agreed to deliver it to them. At the time, I'd still been reeling from the shock of the divorce proceedings, and I'd had no plans to move. It would have been a simple task to load the painting into my SUV to deliver it in person. Now, it wasn't so simple.

I'd never shipped an oil painting before, and I feared that it could be damaged if it wasn't properly crated to protect it during the twelve-hundred-mile trip back to Kansas City. My fear wasn't completely without foundation. With horror, I remembered the afternoon a friend and I had spent picking little bits of Styrofoam packing peanuts off an oil painting that her cousin had sent her, innocently entrusting a packaging store to box and ship it. During transport, the oil paint had warmed enough to become tacky, and we were never able to remove all the residue from its surface.

Pondering my dilemma, I decided to ask some of the co-op members to recommend a shipping service that specialized in transporting artwork, although the down side was that it was bound to be expensive, but I could see no other alternative if I wanted the painting to arrive safely at its destination. Quite a few Roadrunner artists specialized in oil painting, although I couldn't remember any of their names offhand, even though Susan had introduced me to several members on the evening we'd set up our displays for the month.

I kept my computer and my color printer, which I used very sparingly due to the exorbitant price of ink cartridges, on a small desk in the studio. I plugged the cable from my camera into a slot on the back of the PC and uploaded the photos I'd just taken. I'd need to send some pictures to my clients, along with my final invoice, but I wanted to nail down my shipping arrangements first. I looked forward to finalizing the transaction because the last half of their payment would be due as soon as I sent them an invoice, plumping up my dwindling checking account by a welcome two thousand dollars.

As I sorted and viewed the photos I'd just taken on my monitor, I selected the best ones and placed them in a new download folder so I could easily locate them. I felt pleased by how well the painting conveyed the essence of the wooded landscape that my customers had commissioned me to paint, the view they saw from the back porch of their vacation cabin in the Ozarks.

The couple had loved the dreamlike quality of my expressionistic paintings. Decades after I'd studied art in college, I'd finally developed my own unique style. After Crystal Star had seen my paintings at a local outdoors art fair, she'd approached me about scheduling a one-woman show.

Her invitation to show my paintings at her gallery had bolstered my budding confidence in myself as an artist, and the months I'd spent making new artwork for the show were among the happiest of my life. Ned had agreed that I could take time off from the insurance agency to prepare for the show. In fact, he'd agreed readily, and I'd felt grateful for his support. It wasn't until later that it had dawned on me that he'd had an ulterior motive. With my absence from the insurance office, he'd be there alone with his assistant Candy. Long story, short: now they were married and had a baby.

Chapter 8

Laddie heard a noise before the doorbell rang, and he jumped up to wait for me at the front door, tail wagging, eager to greet a new visitor. Since I wasn't expecting anyone, and I remembered Greg's warning about keeping my doors locked, I looked through the peephole to see who stood outside.

My anxiety subsided the instant I recognized my visitor.

"Hello, Officer Dyson," I said, as I opened the door.

He took off his hat and patted Laddie on the head as the curious retriever poked his nose over the threshold.

"Nice dog," he commented, squatting to Laddie's level and scratching him behind the ears. Of course, Laddie couldn't get enough of it, so I finally called a halt since Officer Dyson didn't seem to be in any great hurry to tell me the reason for his visit.

"Come in," I invited, and he stepped inside.

He stared at the floor while he mumbled something about coming down to the station with him.

I wasn't sure I'd heard him correctly.

"What was that, officer?" I asked.

He looked up, sighed, and told me that Lieutenant Belmont wanted me to come down to the station to make an official statement.

"All right. I can come now. Let me just grab my car keys."

"Uh, he said I should bring you."

"And you'll be in trouble if you don't," I guessed.

"That's about the size of it."

"Well, no matter. I'll come along with you, then." I picked up my purse and told Laddie to stay and be a good boy, before locking the front door on my way out.

Officer Dyson opened the passenger door of the police car for me, and I slipped into the front seat. I was glad he hadn't asked me to sit in the back. I had visions of prisoners being hauled to the station in handcuffs, languishing in the back seat.

I was struck by how young he looked, so I asked him how long he'd been on the force.

"Almost a year now, ma'am. They hired me right after I got my associate's degree in criminal justice."

I did some quick calculations and figured he was probably twenty-one or twenty-two, assuming he'd taken two years to obtain his degree and had enrolled in college right away after graduating from high school.

"Please call me Amanda," I said. "'Ma'am' makes me feel so old."

"I'm sorry, ma' . . . uh, Amanda, and you can call me Mike. Officer Dyson sounds so formal."

"It's a deal, Mike," I said, smiling at him. "I suppose we didn't meet under very good circumstances. Last week you stopped me for speeding, and then you responded first when Susan and I found Janice. My neighbor told me she's lived here ten years, and she can't remember there ever being a murder in town."

"She could be right, but I really don't know. I'm from Phoenix myself. Actually, I have my application in with the Phoenix P.D."

"Sounds as though you'll be leaving us soon."

"I hope so," he said. "Uh, I didn't mean it the way it sounded, but I'd really like to move back to Phoenix. My family and friends are there. Besides, Lieutenant Belmont treats all the patrol officers like they're his personal servants, and I'm getting fed up with it."

The gruff Belmont hadn't made a very good impression on me, either, so I could see his point.

When we arrived at the police station, Mike asked me to wait in the lobby for the detective, so I took a seat on one of the orange hard-plastic chairs that provided the only touch of color in the drab reception area. After about five minutes, Mike returned and asked me to come with him. He led me to a small gray room in the back. It was remarkable in that the walls, table, and chairs were all gray. I'd never seen such a dull, depressing room in my life.

"Belmont should be here in a minute," Mike said.

"You mean Lieutenant Belmont, don't you?" the detective growled, coming up behind Mike.

"Yes, sir, lieutentant," Mike responded crisply and left before the detective had a chance to say anything else. I remembered that he had called Mike "Dyson" that very morning, so it seemed that respect only went one way from his point of view.

"I need your statement about what happened this morning. Start from the beginning, and don't leave anything out. Write it down," he directed, handing me some lined notebook paper and a pen. He left abruptly, closing the door behind him.

I decided I didn't want to linger there any longer than necessary, so I began rapidly scribbling my statement. Since there wasn't much to tell, I finished in a few minutes. I went out, into the hallway, to look for the detective to let him know

I'd completed my task, but it was deserted, so I went back to the reception area, where I spotted Sergeant Martinez. He hadn't been there earlier, when I'd arrived with Mike, but he saw me and smiled. It was good to see a friendly face. I told him that I'd finished writing my statement and asked him if I needed to wait for Lieutenant Belmont.

Sergeant Martinez nodded. "He'll need you to sign your statement. Do you have it with you? I have to type it first."

"I left it in the conference room."

"Mrs. Trent," the detective bellowed from down the hallway. I turned to face him. He did not look like a happy camper, as he motioned me to come back to the conference room.

"Where do you think you're going?" he demanded. "I told you to wait for me in the conference room."

"No, you didn't," I disagreed. "I was looking for you, as a matter of fact. Sergeant Martinez told me he has to type my statement before I can sign it."

"You let me worry about that." He ushered me back into the cell-like conference room.

"Wait here," he commanded, before grabbing my handwritten statement and stalking out.

"We're not done yet," he said when he returned. "Why didn't you tell me you had a grudge against Janice Warren?"

"What? That's not true!" I protested. "I hardly knew her."

"Do you deny that you were displeased with the way she conducted your interview for the gallery?"

"Well, I was surprised that the committee members didn't act friendly during my interview," I admitted, taken aback. "But there were three of them, not just Janice, and, anyway, they did accept my application for membership, so I really had no reason to be unhappy."

"So you say."

"It's the truth. I wanted to join the gallery co-op, and I was able to do that. Why would I bear Janice a grudge?"

"You tell me."

"I already told you. I didn't!" I said in frustration.

"You had an argument with her a few days ago."

"No, I didn't."

"You're claiming that you didn't have words with her Saturday evening?"

"We had a discussion about framing my artwork. It wasn't an argument."

"You were fuming, according to witnesses."

Fuming? I wondered how he'd arrived at that conclusion and who the witnesses were. As far as I knew, nobody had overheard my conversation with Janice, but other members may have noticed that she was talking with me, and I remembered turning red with embarrassment because, at the time, I hadn't wanted to reveal too much about my financial status, but she'd kept pushing.

"That's not true, either. Janice suggested I frame my paintings, and I told her I'd consider it, but I couldn't afford the extra expense at the moment."

A tap on the door sounded, and Sergeant Martinez came in, handed the detective my statement, and left, closing the door behind him.

"Read that and sign it."

I scanned the document. Although I tried to steady my hand as I signed it, I was trembling. I hoped he hadn't noticed.

"So you didn't resent Janice calling you out in front of all the other members?"

"She didn't 'call me out,' as you put it. I already told you what we discussed."

"You argued with her."

I could feel my face flaming, just as it had when I was talking to Janice. "No, we didn't argue," I insisted, aware that the pitch of my voice had risen. "If you're implying that I had reason to kill Janice, you're way off base. As I said before, I barely knew her. Why won't you listen to me?"

"I'll ask the questions here."

"Am I under arrest?" I asked abruptly.

"No."

"In that case, I'm going to go home now." I'd had my fill of the lieutenant and his ridiculous insinuations.

"I advise against leaving now. It's to your advantage to cooperate with the police."

"I have cooperated. I've told you everything I know." I grabbed my purse and fled. I could hear him calling my name as I speed walked down the hallway, but he didn't follow me.

Outside, I dug in my purse for my car keys, forgetting briefly that Mike had given me a ride to the station. I certainly wasn't going to go back in and look for him. I would have called Belle for a ride, but she wasn't able to drive yet. I could either call a car service or walk the three miles home. After thinking about it, I decided that the long walk would give me a chance to clear my head, so I hurried to the end of the block and turned the corner onto Main Street.

The first person I saw was Susan, sitting on one of the benches the Chamber of Commerce had provided. There was a pile of used tissues next to her, and she was dabbing at her eyes with another one as I joined her.

"Susan, are you OK? Can I get you a bottle of water or something?"

"Oh, hi, Amanda." She hiccuped. "Thanks, but I'll calm

down in a minute. It's just that horrible man, that Lieutenant Belmont. I think he suspects me of killing Janice."

"You must have just come from the police station."

"Yes. He questioned me for what seemed like hours, but I see now it was less than an hour," she said, glancing at her phone to check the time. "It certainly felt like forever, though. Oh, I can't believe this."

"Neither can I. He questioned me, too. He twisted everything around. I told him I barely knew Janice, but he thinks I bore her a grudge. He kept trying to get me to say that I argued with her. After a while, I couldn't take it anymore, so I left."

"You mean before he was done?"

"Yes. I asked him if I was under arrest, and he said 'no.' I was hoping that all those detective shows I used to watch with my son had it right—that the police can't detain you if you haven't been arrested."

"Wow," Susan said, brightening. "That's great!" She looked at me in admiration. "I wish I'd had the nerve to do what you did. I waited until he told me I could go, but, at the same time, he warned me that he'd have more questions later."

"It might not have been the smartest move I've ever made," I admitted. "He may have it in for me even more now. I don't really understand why he's focusing on us. Just because we found Janice's body doesn't make us killers."

"Especially you, since you just met her last week. Unfortunately, Janice and I had a history of disagreements over the years, mostly when I was still a board member. Somehow, he found out about it, and he kept peppering me with questions about every little squabble. It's like you said: he made each disagreement we had about gallery policies sound like World

War III. By the time he finished interrogating me, I'd convinced myself that he was about to read me my rights."

Evidently, I wasn't the only one who'd been watching detective shows.

Chapter 9

When I told Susan I was going to walk home, she urged me to wait for Chip, who was on his way to pick her up. She said they would be happy to drop me off at my house, but I declined her offer, explaining that the walk would do me good.

The first mile was pleasant enough, as I walked past the boutiques, galleries, and restaurants that lined Main Street; admired their window displays; and paused to read the menu boards the restaurants had set up on the sidewalk to entice passersby to stop and have a bite.

Lonesome Valley enjoyed a large influx of tourists, who kept the local economy humming, and the unique businesses along Main Street were prime attractions, along with art events, a five-star resort hotel on the outskirts of town, and the annual Festival of the West. Each well-attended event drew crowds, eager to spend some of their cash in our community. I knew about the events, not because I'd experienced them yet, but because I'd done my homework before I'd chosen Lonesome Valley as my new home.

After I left Main Street behind and started up the hill towards my house, the walk became more strenuous. After a few blocks, I felt winded and paused to catch my breath.

"Amanda!" I looked toward the street. Belle's husband Dennis, in his red Ford pick-up, had pulled over to the curb. "Need a ride?"

"Thanks, Dennis," I said gratefully, as I climbed into the truck. "This hill doesn't seem nearly as steep when I'm driving."

He laughed. At seventy, Belle's husband was a handsome man with only a few wrinkles, although he did have white hair.

"I wanted to thank you for everything you've done for Belle, especially since I can't be home to help her when I'm working."

"You're entirely welcome. She'd do the same for me; in fact, she invited me for lunch earlier today, and we polished off the last of the frittata you made for breakfast."

He nodded. "She told me what happened at the gallery. That must have been awful for you and your friend to find the poor lady dead."

"It was. The police questioned us at the station, and the detective in charge treated both of us like suspects."

Dennis frowned.

"What is it?" I asked.

"The detective—is he about fifty-five or so? Looks like an unmade bed?

"Right. Do you know him?"

"Unfortunately, I do. He used to be a customer at the feed store, and we were in the same photography club for a while. The man was so unpleasant that we asked him to resign. He never came into the feed store after that. Guess he took his business elsewhere, but what I wanted to tell you was that he got his licks in by retaliating against everyone in the club. We all ended up with traffic tickets for minor infractions, and some of the members who owned businesses received code violation notices citing insignificant issues. Even though I don't own the feed store, we got a couple infraction notices, too, one for parking our truck twenty inches from the curb, instead of eighteen or less. Even though every citation was technically correct, they were all matters that any other cop would have ignored. One guy got a ticket for jaywalking when he crossed the street in front of his house to return a hand saw he'd borrowed from his neighbor, and the street's a dead end with hardly any traffic on it."

I groaned. "And I just walked out on him when he was questioning me. He was so unreasonable."

Dennis's frown deepened. "He's one man you don't want to get on the wrong side of, that's for sure."

"What do you think I should do?"

"Probably best to steer clear of him, if it's possible."

"He may try to call me in again. Maybe I should think about consulting a lawyer."

"I sure hope you don't need one. Too bad he's in charge of the investigation."

I realized that I might have made an enemy when I walked out on Lieutenant Belmont, and now that I'd learned about Dennis's experience with him, I feared the detective might find some way to harass me, since he was inclined to carry a grudge, the very thing he'd accused me of not an hour earlier.

Declining Dennis's invitation to join Belle and him for dinner, I thanked him again for the ride and headed across the front yard to my house.

I felt like getting in bed and pulling a blanket over my head to shut out the world, but, of course, that wouldn't work; besides, my pets would be eagerly awaiting my arrival and their dinners. As soon as I entered my house, I plopped down on a low footstool and embraced my pets. The three of us snuggled for a few minutes before Mona Lisa began meowing loudly and Laddie started prancing in circles, a sure sign that he expected me to take action. I obliged them both, and soon they were gobbling the food I'd dished out in their bowls, while I ate some leftovers for my own dinner. I was still so keyed up, I barely tasted it.

When my phone rang, I braced for the worst, fearing the detective might be calling, but I was relieved to see Susan's picture pop up.

"I have good news and bad news," she informed me without preamble.

I braced for the bad news, but it turned out not to be so bad, after all.

"Evidently, we're not the only people that horrible detective has been talking to. I've already heard from several gallery members he questioned today, and he treated them all just as rudely as he treated us."

"Hmm. That must mean that he wasn't necessarily singling us out. Maybe he doesn't suspect us at all."

"That's kind of what I thought, too," Susan said. "The other thing is that the police won't tell us when we can re-open the gallery. One of our longtime members knows the chief of police, so he's volunteered to talk to him to explain how important it is for us to be up and running again soon. We're on the schedule for tours both Friday and Saturday this week. The buses come up from Phoenix with loads of tourists, and their first stop is always right in front of our gallery. We'll miss a lot of business if we can't open, and I know that's what Janice would have wanted. She certainly had a head for business, even though it was a hard one. She didn't deserve to be murdered for it, though."

"You think someone killed her just because they didn't like her? That seems awfully extreme."

"I don't know, but she did have a way of getting under your skin. Maybe she pushed the wrong person too far. She could be relentless, and many of the members were frenemies, rather than friends."

"Why didn't the members vote her out, if she was so unpopular? Surely, there are plenty of other people who could take on the job of gallery director."

"Like I said, she knows business, but, more important, she owns our building. We get the gallery space rent free."

Chapter 10

"No wonder she acted like she owned the place," I said. "She really *did* own the place."

"Not only that, but she donated her services as director," Susan added. "The co-op never paid her a penny."

"Is that the reason the gallery takes no commission on sales? When I first found out about the no-commission policy, I thought it was unusual, but a great perk."

"That's right. We're the only co-op gallery I know of that operates without taking a percentage of sales. The wall space rental and our annual dues cover all our expenses. But, I'm getting off track. One of the reasons I called you was to let you know about our members meeting tomorrow night. We need to make some decisions fast. We'll hold the meeting at the gallery if the police let us back in by then. If not, Pamela's arranged for us to use the library's meeting room. I'll let you know which place tomorrow as soon as we find out for sure. Can you attend?"

"Yes. I'll be there. How often do you usually have meetings?"

"Normally, only twice a year. I wish your first meeting could be under better circumstances. We usually ask new members to stand and give a little talk about their artwork, but it will have to wait until the next meeting."

"No problem," I said, with relief. Public speaking has never been my forté.

"Well, I'd better go. I have a few more calls to make, but let me know if Lieutenant Belmont tries to ask you any more questions."

"I will," I assured her. Despite what she'd told me earlier, I could tell that Susan was still concerned that we might be more than minor blips on the detective's radar.

I spent the rest of the evening calling Emma, Dustin, and my parents to let them know about the day's tragedy. Although it seemed unlikely they'd hear the news elsewhere, since it wasn't a national story, I didn't want to take the slightest chance that they might hear about it from anybody but me. Predictably, my family was shocked and worried about me. Emma and Dustin both offered to rush to Lonesome Valley to lend me moral support, and my parents pleaded with me to visit them in Florida until the murderer was arrested. It took me a while to convince Emma and Dustin that their moral support could be given via phone. It was more difficult to persuade my parents, probably because I'll always be the baby of the family from their point of view.

I'd hoped telling the story again and again would help me come to terms with discovering Janice's body, but it had the opposite effect. I spent the night tossing and turning so much that my affable golden boy moved from the bed, where he normally warmed my feet, to a nearby chair, and Mona Lisa, who usually curled up on a pillow beside me, deserted me, too.

When I dragged out of bed in the morning, I felt as though I hadn't slept at all, but I must have because I woke up when Laddie nudged my arm with his nose. At first, I resisted, but I finally gave in to his doggie persistence. After our usual flurry of routine early morning activity, I forced myself to stop procrastinating, which was my very worst habit as an artist, and get some painting done. I usually had two or three projects in the works, but since I'd just finished the commissioned landscape for the judge and his wife and had only one other canvas I was currently working on, it was time to start some new paintings.

I'd gessoed several canvases a week earlier so that the prep work would already be done when I was ready to start my next new paintings. I set two of the canvases on easels, selected the colors for my underpainting and thinned the paints so that the bottom layer would dry more quickly. My underpainting completely covered each canvas, establishing the preliminary balance and mood of the work. I often concentrated on shaping three main areas—earth, sky, and trees, but those would come to life later. Subsequent layers obliterated the underpainting, but I always found that it helped me establish the mood I wanted to evoke when prospective customers looked at the finished painting.

When I'd finished underpainting both canvases, I went on to my partially finished canvas, where I worked with thicker paint, combining and blending the colors I applied right to the canvas, rather than on my palette. I stepped back and looked at the ethereal scene with a critical eye and decided it was shaping up nicely.

By the time Susan's text came through, notifying me that our meeting would be held at seven in the library meeting room, I'd painted for several hours, walked Laddie and Mr. Big, exchanged casseroles with Belle, and mopped the floor.

I was feeling rather pleased with myself for my productive day as I dressed for the meeting in tan linen pants and a fuchsia knit top and draped a colorful silk scarf I'd tie dyed around my neck. I checked my hair and make-up with a hand mirror, twirling around so that I could see the sides and back of my hair in another mirror. That's when I saw the long gray hair curling around the back of my ear.

Immediately, I pulled it out with a sharp tug. I'd been finding more and more of those pesky gray hairs lately, just another reminder that I'd soon be reaching the half century mark, even though I felt considerably younger. People used to tell me how young I looked, but I hadn't heard any such comments for several months now. I thought the upheaval of my divorce had probably taken its toll.

I left some lights on in both the studio and my little home, assured my pets that I'd be back later, and gave the side door to the carport a tug on my way out, just to make sure it was properly locked.

When I arrived at the library, I found its small parking lot packed. I parked on the street about a block away and hurried to arrive at the meeting on time. I rushed into the room where the gallery members had gathered at exactly six fifty-nine, but I wasn't the last to arrive. A young couple with a baby in tow came in after me and sat in the back row. I guessed they'd chosen the spot so that, if the baby started to fuss or cry, they could make a quick exit.

I took a seat close to the front so that I'd be able to see what was going on there. As I sandwiched myself between a young woman with black curly hair who looked as though she were still in high school and an elderly man whose blue eyes were still bright behind the thick lenses of his eyeglasses, I spotted Susan sitting a couple rows in front of me on the aisle. At the same time, she turned to look around, saw me, and waved.

My neighbors and I hardly had a chance to introduce ourselves to each other before Pamela called the meeting to order. She began by telling us that she didn't yet have any information about funeral arrangements for Janice, but she'd notify all the members as soon as she found out. Before she continued the meeting, she called for a moment of silence to remember Janice. She cut the moment short after about fifteen seconds, and it was clear she wanted to get down to business.

"We've just received word that we'll be able to open the gallery Friday morning as usual." Scattered clapping erupted at the announcement, perhaps unseemly under the circumstances, I thought, although I could understand the members wanting to resume business as usual.

"We have Ralph Anderson to thank for pleading our case with the chief of police and explaining how important it is for us to be open on the weekend," Pamela continued. She scanned the crowd, "Ralph, where are you?"

The old man sitting next to me rose, nodded to the other members, and quickly sat down again.

"Our original work schedule for the gallery will be in effect, so if you're supposed to work Friday, just come in as usual. I'll be there to open," Pamela announced.

A heavyset woman with long red hair interrupted. "Shouldn't we get the locks changed? Who knows how many keys are floating around? We haven't installed new locks since I've been a member."

"That's a good point, Carrie," Chip said. "I'll take care of it."

"Thank you, Ch—Travis," Pamela said. "Now for the next item on the agenda: we need a new gallery director. Nobody can really fill Janice's shoes, but I'm willing to step in."

"Wait a minute," the man in the back row who'd come in after me with his wife and baby said, standing. "I think we should hear from some other people before we just coronate you."

Whoa! There must be some history between those two, I thought.

"What about the rest of you board members?" he continued.

"Personally, I think we should be grateful to Pamela for volunteering," Chip said. "I certainly don't have time to do it."

"Too busy delivering pizzas," someone in back of me whispered, and a few people nearby snickered, but the rest of the group didn't hear the mean-spirited jibe.

"Well, what about Valerie or Frank?" the man pressed.

"Oh, come on, Lonnie. You know we both teach full-time at the high school."

"Janice's replacement wouldn't have to be a board member. What about some of the rest of you members?" Lonnie looked around the room for some back-up. "Ralph, you could do it. You're one of the gallery's founders."

"Well," Ralph hesitated. "I don't know."

"Excuse me. Excuse me." The loud voice came from the back of the meeting room. As the woman who'd spoken bustled to the front, the crowd emitted a universal gasp. Her entrance would have been even more dramatic if she hadn't stumbled on her way to the podium.

She looked very much like Janice, although her hair was blond, and, unlike Janice, she wore heavy make-up. I realized she must be Judith, Janice's sister. Rebecca hadn't mentioned that they were identical, but the family resemblance was so striking, despite their different hair styles, hair color, and make-up, that I thought they must be twins.

"I'm Judith Warren, Janice's sister and sole heir," she declared, quickly recovering her footing.

Her announcement didn't take long to sink in.

"You own the gallery building," Frank stated flatly.

"Yes."

"Are you planning to sell it?" Valerie asked.

"I have no plans at present to sell. I'll be moving into Janice's apartment on the second floor in a few days. For now, I'm staying at the Lonesome Valley Resort. Like my sister, I've been involved in the art gallery business for years. I owned the Texican Gallery in Austin, which I recently sold, so I have no current business obligations. I'd like to volunteer my services as gallery director, at least temporarily."

"What about long term?" Valerie asked.

"We'll see how it goes," she said. "I might be persuaded to make the arrangement permanent."

"Janice never charged us rent for the gallery space," Pamela said. "Are you going to honor her memory and do the same?"

Judith turned to Pamela with a lopsided smile on her face. "I think I'm in the best position to decide how to honor my sister's memory, but, no. For now, everything will remain as Janice left it. I suggest that the membership discuss my proposal and take a vote. If you have any doubts about my credentials, you can Google my name or the Texican Gallery in Austin to confirm my expertise. You know where to reach me."

After Judith left, a stunned silence fell for a few seconds before the members all started talking at once.

"She has us over a barrel," Ralph said. "Just like her sister did."

Valerie opened her laptop and began typing furiously. "She is who she says she is."

"As if there were any doubt," Susan commented. "She looks just like Janice."

"I mean the business angle. She owned the Texican Gallery in Austin for the last twenty years."

"So why did she sell it?" Lonnie asked. "How do we know the gallery was run well?"

"According to this article in Austin Business Monthly, the gallery sold for a record price. Nobody's going to pay that kind of money for a gallery if there's something wrong with it."

"Anyway, you wanted someone else to be gallery director," Pamela said pointedly to Lonnie. "Here she is on a silver platter, and if we don't take her up on her offer, we could be out on the street."

Chip reached out and put his hand on Pamela's. "I know we all appreciate Pamela's offer to serve as director, and I know she'd make a great one." As he spoke, Pamela slowly withdrew her hand from under his. "But, she's right. We're under the gun here. I think we should accept Judith's offer for now. We can always rescind it later. I don't know about you, but I'm looking forward to a busy weekend at the gallery."

"I agree," Frank said. "With all the tourists due in over the weekend, we might as well strike while the iron's hot. I move that we appoint Judith Warren temporary gallery director."

And that was that.

The motion was quickly seconded, the members voted in favor by a wide majority, and the meeting was adjourned.

Susan caught up with me as I was making my way through the crowd, toward the door.

"I almost passed out when Janice's sister showed up," Susan said. "For a minute, I thought I was seeing a ghost."

"I was surprised, too. She looks just like her. They must be twins. Did you get the feeling Judith was enjoying our reaction to her? Like maybe she wanted to shock us?"

"Could be, but why would she want to do that?" Susan asked.

"Because she thinks one of us killed her sister."

Chapter 11

It was well past dark by the time we left the library. Several other gallery members had parked on the street, too, so I joined the group headed west, down the street toward my SUV. Listening to their remarks about the meeting, I gleaned that they were glad the Roadrunner could re-open Friday, and they hoped for a busy weekend. Nobody mentioned Janice or her sister.

Mindful of what Dennis had told me about his experiences with Lieutenant Belmont, I slowly drove home, keeping my speed well under the posted limit. I didn't want to give the detective any reason to issue me a citation.

As I turned the corner onto Canyon Drive, I was surprised to see a car parked in front of my house. I'd left my porch light on when I'd departed for the meeting earlier, and there, sitting on the front steps with his arm draped around Laddie, sat my son. I was so stunned I almost missed the turn into the driveway. I parked short of the carport as Dustin approached with Laddie at his side. He opened the car door for me, and I jumped out with a whoop of joy and hugged him, while Laddie, not to be left out, crowded close to us.

I hadn't seen Dustin since my move to Lonesome Valley.

He'd offered to drive the small rental truck packed with the few belongings I was taking with me, but he'd come down with the flu the day before my departure, so Emma and I had hitched my SUV to the truck, and we'd taken turns driving on the twelve-hundred-mile trip. She'd stayed with me a few days, until her winter holiday break was nearly over, and she'd had to return to college for the spring semester. When we'd said good-bye at the airport in Phoenix, we'd planned for her to come back to Lonesome Valley at the end of the semester to spend the summer with me. Dustin had promised he'd visit in the summer, too, and I hadn't expected to see either of my children until then.

"I'm so happy to see you," I said, "but you didn't need to come right now. Finding a body my first day at the gallery was a real shock, but I'm trying to come to terms with it."

"I'll say it was a shock. Emma was ready to get on the first flight to Phoenix after you talked to her last night, but I convinced her she should stay at school and study since I knew she had two big exams coming up, and I'd already decided to come myself."

"I suppose you talked to grandma and grandpa, too."

Dustin grinned. "I did. I wanted to have my favorite girl all to myself for a few days."

We stayed up late talking, until Dustin started to yawn, and then we took the cushions off the sofa and pulled out the hide-a-bed. When I woke in the morning to Mona Lisa's loud meow, both Dustin and Laddie were gone. I pulled on a robe, fed Mona Lisa, brewed some coffee for Dustin, and made some tea for myself. I was just popping a tin of muffins into the oven when Dustin and Laddie, both panting vigorously, returned from their jog. Laddie flopped down on the hardwood floor while Dustin joined me at the tiny table in the corner of the living room next to the kitchen, which was so small there was no room for a table in it. Dustin drank his coffee, and I sipped my tea before making a mushroom omelet for us to eat with the muffins. Both were a big hit with my son.

"Thanks, Mom," he said as he polished off his third muffin. "This was a real treat. I usually grab a cup of coffee on my way to work. Sometimes people at the office bring in some doughnuts or bagels and leave them in the break room for everybody else, but that doesn't happen too often. Most days, I wait till lunch before I eat anything."

"My pleasure. What would you like to do today?"

"I wouldn't mind having a look at the town. It was dark when I arrived last night. Maybe you could play tour guide."

"All right. Let's do that. We can drive around so you can see Lonesome Valley and some of its landmarks, and then maybe we could browse at a few of the galleries downtown. Don't worry: I won't drag you into any boutiques."

"Sounds good to me. Let's take Laddie with us while we tour. We can stop at a park before we come home and drop him off before we hit the galleries."

"OK, but we should probably bring Mr. Big along with us, too. I've been walking him every day since Belle had her accident, and the little scamp loves the park."

"The more, the merrier," Dustin agreed.

An hour later, the four of us piled into my SUV with Dustin at the wheel. I'd vetoed taking his rental car on our tour since the dogs were coming with us.

As its name suggested, Lonesome Valley did indeed lie in a valley—at least most of the town did. The west side, the residential neighborhood where I lived, was on a slope, and there wasn't much to see there, other than houses, so we proceeded downtown, where I pointed out the Roadrunner and the shops on Main Street, the library, and our town museum. Then we drove to the east side, where there were a couple of small lakes with canoe rentals, hiking trails, bicycle paths, and a huge park, the site of outdoor art fairs and the annual Festival of the West. Next to one of the lakes stood the five-star Lonesome Valley Resort, which boasted upscale restaurants and its own private golf course, along with indoor and outdoor swimming pools, handball and tennis courts, full gym facilities, and a luxurious spa. I'd never been inside the place, but I intended to visit it someday and dine there. As though reading my mind, Dustin suggested that we book a table for dinner at one of the restaurants in the hotel.

"Good idea, but let's do lunch there, instead. I have to work at the gallery from nine to one tomorrow, so we could go right after I'm done."

"OK, but what about tonight?"

"Belle and Dennis invited us for a barbecue, unless you'd rather not go. The weather's so nice, we'll be able to sit outside on their patio."

"That's fine with me."

"Good. I'll let Belle know that we're on. Sorry I forgot to check with you earlier."

"No problem. I'll make us lunch reservations for tomorrow at the resort. Shall we go over to the park now? These dogs are getting restless. I think they know where we're headed."

After a romp in the dog park and a walk around its perimeter, Laddie and Mr. Big were ready to go home for an afternoon nap. We dropped them off and drove back downtown for our gallery tour.

I always enjoyed looking at other artists' work, and most of the galleries on Main Street changed their exhibits fairly often, so there was always something new to see. Some of the galleries featured work from only one artist, but most of the others represented several artists. I'd thought about seeking representation from one of them, but the fifty-percent commission that constituted a gallery's share of sales certainly didn't compare favorably to the no-commission sales at the Roadrunner. I'd figured that, even with the monthly wall rental fee and the annual membership dues, I'd come out ahead at our co-op gallery, assuming that my artwork sold.

We lingered a while in a tiny gallery where acrylic paintings of brightly colored blossoms caught my eye. They were so delicate and pretty, I couldn't resist buying some of the artist's printed floral note cards. Because note cards are the least expensive item artists can make available, many artists sell them to customers who like their artwork but may not want to make a costlier purchase. I tucked the little packet of cards into my purse and suggested that we visit the few galleries that weren't on Main Street.

The first gallery where we stopped featured comic book art, while the second specialized in abstract, steel, tabletop sculptures. Dustin claimed he had no artistic talent, but he had a good eye for all kinds of art, and I could tell that he especially enjoyed both of these off-the-beaten-path galleries.

"One more, and then we'll end our tour," I said, after Dustin had finished a lively conversation with the artist who fabricated the steel sculptures.

"Lead on, Mom."

"OK. I've never been in this next gallery, but I think it's about half a block down, on the other side of the street."

We crossed First Street and found the Brooks Miller Gallery. As soon as we entered, a thirtyish woman with long blond hair greeted Dustin. The lifestyle in Lonesome Valley tended to be casual, as was the way residents customarily dressed, but this woman wore gold jewelry with her red silk shantung dress, and the red soles of her spikey Louboutins matched her dress perfectly. She took one look at the pair of us and immediately zeroed in on my son, ignoring me completely. I noticed Dustin didn't object as she linked arms with him and led him toward a group of paintings at the back of the gallery. Her maneuver left me free to wander around the large space, and I was dumbfounded by what I saw. All the paintings were abstract. I like abstract art, so there was nothing objectionable about that, but I found the ugly color palette the artist favored almost nauseating and the composition of his pieces terrible. I wondered whether the gallery ever sold any of these works. Perhaps, I speculated, the so-called artist was wealthy enough to afford to maintain a vanity gallery.

I could hear the woman's high-powered sales pitch and see Dustin gazing at her in fascination. Despite his obvious attraction to her, I knew she was wasting her breath trying to sell him a painting. I caught a slight whiff of her perfume as the pair returned to the front of the gallery. She pressed her business card into Dustin's hand as he thanked her for showing him the gallery's artwork. We left without her ever having acknowledged my presence.

"Earth to Dustin," I said as we walked back toward Main Street.

"Oh, sorry, Mom," he apologized. "Isn't she beautiful? She gave me her card. Do you suppose she wants me to call her?"

"Could I see her card?"

"Sure," he said, handing it to me. On the back, she had written "Darkness at Dawn" and "Special Price, $2000."

"I hate to burst your bubble, Dustin, but I think she wants to sell you a painting," I said, pointing to the note on the back of the card.

"Oh, yeah." He didn't seem the least bit deterred. "I think I'll call her anyway."

I knew better than to try to persuade him otherwise, so I changed the subject. "What did you think of the Brooks Miller art?"

"Oh, I thought it was really bad. How about you?"

"Awful. Just awful." I was about to say that it was a shame we'd ended our tour of downtown on a sour note, but I realized Dustin didn't feel the same. "Let's stop at the grocery store on the way home. I want to make a pie to take to the barbecue."

"Chocolate meringue?"

His face fell when I told him I was thinking of apple.

"I'm teasing," I declared. "Of course, chocolate meringue. I'll make two pies—one to take to Belle and Dennis's and one for us.

"Thanks, Mom!" His sad face transformed into a dreamy expression. I hoped he was thinking about my chocolate meringue pie, not the beautiful saleswoman from the Brooks Miller Gallery, but I feared it was more likely the latter.

Back at home, I got to work, mixing the pie dough and preparing the filling. I had to shoo Laddie out of the kitchen more than once as I beat the egg whites to stiff peaks. There was hardly room for one person in the tiny kitchen, let alone one adult and a large dog, so Dustin volunteered to play fetch with Laddie in the backyard while I finished my baking.

I'd just removed both pies from the oven and placed them

on racks to cool when the doorbell rang.

I swung the front door open, and Chip was standing there, holding a pizza box and grinning.

"Hi," he said, stepping inside, although I hadn't invited him to come in. "I thought you might like to have dinner with me. I brought us a pizza—veggie supreme, just like you and your neighbor ordered the other day."

"How did you know where I live?" I asked, hoping Susan hadn't told him.

"You're in our member directory."

"Oh."

Before I had a chance to say more, Dustin and Laddie burst in. Dustin looked at the pizza box.

"Was the barbecue canceled?" he asked.

"Uh, no," I said. "Dustin, this is Travis—Chip, from the Roadrunner. Chip, my son Dustin."

Chip set the pizza box on the table and shook hands with Dustin. Neither one of them looked too happy.

"Well, it sounds as though you two already have dinner plans," Chip said. "We can do it another time."

Dustin raised his eyebrows at this statement while I picked up the pizza box from the table and handed it back to Chip.

"See you at the gallery," he said as he left, taking his pizza with him.

"Did you forget you had a date with that guy, Mom?"

"Of course not. I didn't have a clue that he was going to show up. I certainly didn't invite him. Why would he do that, anyway?"

"He likes you, Mom."

"But that's ridiculous! He's way too young for me, even if I were interested in dating, which I most definitely am not. He's your age. Literally, he's young enough to be my son."

"I have a feeling the age difference isn't going to stop him. You'll probably have to tell him you're not interested."

"Oh, great," I groaned. The thought of having to fend off a would-be admirer didn't appeal to me in the least. Maybe I should have felt flattered, but I felt put upon, instead. I hadn't done a thing to encourage Chip's unwelcome attention. Not only that, but I was far from pleased that he'd shown up on my doorstep out of the blue. In fact, I was more than a little freaked out that he'd tracked down my address.

So far, my move to Lonesome Valley had resulted in more than a few unpleasant experiences. I fervently hoped Chip's visit would be the last.

Chapter 12

When I arrived at the gallery the next morning to meet Susan, Chip and another man, carrying a tool box, stood outside the door. A locksmith's van was parked across the street.

I stepped out of my car, and Susan joined me, but before we had a chance to go inside, a large black SUV double-parked in front of the gallery, and Judith got out. The driver pulled two suitcases from the back and set them on the sidewalk in front of the gallery.

"Changing the locks, I see," she said. "Can we limit the key distribution to the board members?"

"That's the plan," Chip said, grabbing the handles of Judith's suitcases. "I'll take these up to the apartment for you. I'd suggest that you change the lock on the apartment door, too. In fact, you may want to consider staying someplace else for a while. The police haven't arrested anyone yet for Janice's murder."

"I'm aware of that, but I prefer to stay here. I'm not without protection." Beckoning us to come closer, she opened her large shoulder bag, revealing a handgun tucked inside.

Susan and I gasped, but Chip took the startling revelation in stride. The locksmith, absorbed in his task, didn't seem to be paying any attention.

"All right, then," Chip said. "I can see that your mind's made up. Let's drop off these suitcases upstairs. We need to open the gallery in a few minutes."

Judith followed Chip inside.

"I wonder if she has a permit for that thing," I said to Susan.

"She doesn't need one," the locksmith answered. He'd seen the gun, after all.

"Really?" I said skeptically. "For a concealed weapon? I know Arizona's an open carry state, but . . . ."

"It's true," Susan told me. "Janice had a gun, too, but it didn't help her. She obviously had her back turned when she was attacked. She must have known someone was behind her, but she wasn't frightened of whoever it was. That's what I think, anyway."

"Makes sense," I murmured as we went inside.

As soon as Judith and Chip returned, Judith went straight to the locksmith and instructed him to change the locks on the second-floor apartment door.

"We can't get into the apartment," Chip told Susan and me while Judith talked to the locksmith. "I thought the front door key to the gallery also worked for Janice's apartment, but it doesn't anymore. She must have had her own lock changed, I guess, but she never mentioned it."

The flurry of activity at the front door had distracted us for a few minutes, but Susan suggested that we'd better hurry to prepare for the expected onslaught of tourists who would soon arrive on the first tour bus. Susan whispered to me that Chip had engaged a crew to clean the crime scene early that morning. I nodded, not wanting to think about it. We signed in, and Susan showed me where to find the paperwork and how to process a transaction.

"All our policies and procedures are in this handbook," she said, "but, if you have any questions, just ask me. That's what I'm here for, and don't worry about a thing: you'll never be alone in the gallery. We always have at least two members scheduled to work." She glanced outside. "We're just in the nick of time. Here comes the bus now."

We watched as the tour bus stopped outside the gallery and a crowd of eager tourists disembarked. The locksmith politely held the door open for them before returning to work installing the new lock.

As the crowd scattered about the gallery, Judith, Chip, Susan, and I circulated, answering questions and talking about the artwork on display.

A woman expressed interest in one of my paintings, a landscape of a lake with a grove of trees in the foreground. I felt disappointed when she said she'd "think about it" after I offered to take it off the wall and write up the sale.

When my prospective customer left, I found myself alone in the back area with Judith, who was looking at the empty pedestal where Janice's bear had been displayed.

"Did we sell a sculpture?" she asked me.

"No, I'm afraid not. One of your sister's sculptures used to be there—a bronze bear."

"Well, where is it now? Did someone put it back in her apartment?"

"The police have it. They said it was evidence. I found it lying on the floor the day she . . . ."

Judith held up her hand. She'd heard enough. "So they think it's the murder weapon?"

"Possibly. I really don't know."

Without a word, she turned and left the area. In a few

minutes, she came back. When I saw what she was carrying, I couldn't believe it.

"Where did you find it?" I asked, amazed. "I thought the police still had it."

"Don't be silly," she sniffed. "This bear's obviously one of a limited edition, number seven to be precise. It was in Janice's office."

"So the other bear was number six," I speculated.

"Not necessarily. Janice sold her work in other galleries, besides the Roadrunner. I'm sure the records will be around here somewhere."

She placed the new bear on the pedestal, moving it around until she was satisfied that it was displayed to its best advantage.

The rush of tourists seemed to be over. Most of them had moved to other attractions on Main Street. Susan and Chip stood near the check-out counter, where a few customers had stopped to pay for their purchases on the way out.

"How did we do?" I asked them.

"I sold one of my small papier mâché animals," Susan said, "and one of Carrie's turquoise necklaces."

"I didn't sell a thing," Chip said, "but Judith sold one of Ralph's huge oil paintings. I'm going to put the sold sign on it now."

Curious to see the painting, I followed Chip. Perfectly executed in the realistic style, Ralph's expensive artwork depicted a mountain scene at sunset.

"Ralph's going to be happy," Chip said.

"I'll say," I agreed, glancing at the price as Chip placed the sold sign next to the painting. "I hope the buyer's not planning on hauling this one back on the bus."

Chip laughed. "No way. He said it would fit in his truck.

He's going to pick it up later. By the way, I didn't mean to upset your son last night. I didn't realize he lives with you."

"He's visiting," I said automatically and almost instantly regretted telling Chip, because he winked at me.

I pretended not to notice and excused myself, saying I needed to check with Susan about my schedule. The timing hadn't seemed right to tell Chip I wasn't interested in him. Besides, despite Dustin's opinion, I wasn't one hundred percent sure that Chip really found me attractive. Maybe he was just a friendly, if somewhat flirtatious, guy. If that were the case, I'd feel like a fool if I brought up the subject before he did.

Around eleven, another bus drove up, and, again, the tourists flocked into the gallery, keeping us busy. Although nobody bought any of my own paintings, I sold a small painting of a horse by another artist and a larger abstract artwork. Lonnie, the man who had objected to Pamela's offer to become gallery director at our meeting, had painted the abstract. I didn't recognize the name of the member who'd painted the horse, and I figured it would take me a while to connect names with faces, even though I'd met, or had at least seen, most of the co-op's members, either when I'd hung my display or at the meeting.

By quarter to one, the tourists had cleared out of the gallery, Judith had gone upstairs to Janice's apartment, and Chip had made a food run to pick up some lunch for Susan, who would be staying for the afternoon. When I left at one, some of the other members were due to come in to staff the gallery.

I was killing time, browsing the jewelry display case near the check-out counter, when the woman who'd admired my lake painting earlier returned and told me she'd decided to buy it. Although it was a small work and one of my more inexpensive pieces, I was delighted to have sold a painting the first day I worked in the gallery.

Maybe things were looking up, after all.

Chapter 13

Cabo at the Lonesome Valley Resort lived up to its reputation, both for its cuisine and its ambiance. The attentive wait staff made sure we never lacked anything. Dustin and I were lingering over chocolate mousse and coffee when a distinguished-looking man about my age entered the restaurant. Unlike Cabo's customers, who were dressed casually, he wore a suit and tie. He stopped at the table closest to the entrance and talked to the patrons briefly before going to the next table and doing the same. After several minutes, he made his way to our table.

"I hope everything's to your satisfaction," he said.

"Yes. The restaurant is lovely," I replied.

"Excellent food, too," Dustin added.

"I'm glad you're enjoying it. Where are you folks from?"

"My son's visiting from Kansas City," I said, "but I live here in Lonesome Valley."

"A local? We don't see many of our community's residents here at the Resort. Have you been to the Brooks Miller Gallery downtown, by any chance?"

"Yesterday, as a matter of fact."

"How did you like it?"

Dustin was about to answer when I shot him a look. Luckily,

our twenty-five years of non-verbal communication paid off, and he understood.

"Very interesting," I said diplomatically. I had a feeling we were talking to the man himself, and even though I thought his artwork was terrible, I didn't want to insult him.

"I'm Brooks Miller," he announced proudly.

To divert him from any more discussion about his paintings, I said, "You have such a spacious gallery."

"Yes, the space itself is satisfactory, but the location isn't the best. I wanted a place on Main Street, but, unfortunately, there weren't any available when we opened the gallery last year."

I could tell that Dustin's radar kicked in when he heard Brooks say "we."

"Do you have a partner?" Dustin asked.

"You could say so. My wife manages the gallery while I manage the Resort. It's all I can do to carve out a little bit of time for painting. Well, nice meeting you."

Dustin's glum look said it all.

"I'm sorry, Dustin. I know you like her."

"It's more than that, Mom. I called her this morning while you were working at the gallery and asked her out for dinner tonight. She said she couldn't go to dinner, but she agreed to meet me for a drink when she gets off work at six."

"Oh, Dustin."

"I wonder what her game is, anyway."

Since I'd already told him what I thought she wanted, I didn't comment.

"I could cancel," Dustin said, "but I think I'll go and play along."

I didn't like the sound of that. "Dustin, be careful. You're playing with fire. If Brooks finds out, he's not likely to take too kindly to another man going out with his wife."

"And I'd be doing the same thing Candy did when she made a play for Dad," he said, finally seeing the light. "I'm sorry, Mom. I wasn't thinking straight. I'll text her and cancel."

I hadn't brought up my ex-husband's name since Dustin's arrival. I didn't want to put my children in the middle of an already-awkward situation any more than they already were, and I'd encouraged them to maintain a relationship with their father, but it was difficult. I knew they hadn't forgiven him yet for divorcing me and marrying Candy the minute our divorce was final.

"I saw Dad last weekend," Dustin said, as we walked to the car. "I didn't know if I should mention it."

"It's all right, Dustin." I was beginning to realize that I didn't feel much of anything for my ex-husband anymore.

"I saw the baby. Cute kid, but he's awfully fussy. He cried most of the time while I was there. Dad and Candy looked like they hadn't slept for days. It doesn't seem right that they're living in our house. I think Dad should at least have bought a different house for them to live in."

"He probably can't afford it. The house is already mortgaged to the hilt. He told me it was underwater, that we had no equity at all."

Dustin frowned. "You mean to tell me that Dad didn't buy out your half?"

"He told me there was nothing to buy."

"That doesn't sound right."

"He ought to know. He always handled all our finances."

"Doesn't sound like he was doing a very good job of it," Dustin grumbled.

"Let's not go there. It's a beautiful day, I have a new life here, and my favorite son's visiting me. What could be better? By the way, did I tell you I finished that commissioned work that I painted for the judge and his wife?"

"No, but I saw it in the studio. It's a great painting, Mom."

"Thank you. I'm pleased with it myself. Now the only problem is transporting it back to Kansas City. I want to have the arrangements for the shipping made before I send them the final photos of the painting and my invoice."

"Don't tell me they haven't paid for it yet. And I hope you're charging them for shipping."

"They've paid half. The other half is due when I finish. As for the shipping, I didn't know I'd be moving at the time I took the commission. When I promised to deliver it to them, it didn't occur to me that I might not still be living in Kansas City."

"Shipping's going to take a big bite out of your profit."

"I know, but I can't very well change the terms of our agreement after the fact."

"True."

As soon as we walked in the door at home, we greeted Laddie and Mona Lisa, and Dustin went into the studio, saying he'd like to take a closer look at my landscape.

"You don't happen to have a yardstick or a tape measure, do you, Mom?"

"Sorry, no. A lot of little things like that didn't make it into the truck when I moved, but I'm sure Belle and Dennis have one you could borrow."

"Good idea. I'll go check."

He returned in a few minutes with a metal tape measure in one hand and a plate of Belle's peanut butter cookies in the other. The fact that we'd had lunch topped off with chocolate mousse only an hour earlier hadn't stopped Dustin from sampling Belle's treats.

"Great cookies," he said, setting the plate on the kitchen counter. "Almost as good as yours."

I laughed, "You don't need to butter me up. I already planned to make all your favorites for dinner tonight."

"Thanks, Mom," he said, giving me a peck on the cheek. Laddie followed him into the studio, and I heard Dustin closing the studio door. I looked out the front window, and there were Dustin and Laddie. Dustin lifted the trunk lid, but I couldn't see what he was doing, while Laddie strained at his leash, eager for a jaunt. As soon as Dustin lowered the lid, he put something in his pocket, reached down and adjusted Laddie's leash, and they both took off running down the block. When they returned at a slow jog, Laddie immediately flopped down on the floor, panting happily,

"I hadn't planned on leaving the yard, but Laddie acted like he expected to go somewhere, so I thought I'd take him for a quick run."

"He likes to get out and about. What were you doing, anyway? I saw you looking in the trunk of your rental."

"I had an idea, but I wanted to make sure your painting would fit in the trunk of the car before I said anything."

"If you want to drop it off at a shipper in Phoenix on your way to the airport, I'll need to find a good one. I meant to ask some of the gallery members to recommend a reliable art shipper, but I was so upset by the murder that I forgot all about it. I must be losing it."

"You're not losing it, Mom. It's been a stressful time. I thought I'd deliver the painting in person. I can cancel my flight and call the rental car agency to arrange to return the car in Kansas City, rather than in Phoenix."

"Oh, Dustin, that's sweet of you, but it's too much. Don't you have to work Monday?"

"Yes, but that gives me two days to drive back and deliver your painting. I can leave around noon tomorrow, stop in the evening when I get tired, and drive the rest of the way Sunday. You know I like to drive. I'll listen to some audiobooks and drink plenty of coffee. It's no problem, really, and I'll bet your customers will appreciate getting their painting right away."

"Well, if you're sure . . . ."

"I am, but first they need to pay you their final installment."

"I'm all for that. I'll email them the photos along with my invoice, and they can pay online."

"Ask them if they'll be home to accept delivery Sunday night, too, OK?"

"I'll take care of it right now," I said, reaching for my laptop.

Not five minutes later, a message from PayBuddy popped up informing me that my invoice had been paid. Then my cell phone rang. It was the judge's wife, saying how excited she was that the painting was ready, especially since they would be hosting a party next weekend and they wanted all their friends to see it.

"Is it all right if I give out your phone number? A lot of these people buy art."

I assured her that would be fine before turning the phone over to Dustin so that he could exchange phone numbers and arrange the delivery.

"We're all set," he said as he put my phone down.

I gave him a big hug while Laddie pranced around us, and Mona Lisa, not to be left out, jumped up and draped herself over my shoulder, purring loudly.

Chapter 14

As I waved good-bye to my son the next day, I swiped a tear from the corner of my eye. I felt very much alone. Even though he hadn't lived at home for several years, I was used to seeing him at least once a week. Our Sunday dinners had been a family ritual.

Sensing my mood, Laddie leaned against my leg and nuzzled me, whining softly. I leaned over and ran my hands through his thick, silky fur, telling him what a good boy he was. I thought about taking him for another walk but decided against it, since Justin and I had finished a marathon walk with both Laddie and Mr. Big only an hour earlier.

As we headed back to the house, Belle came out her front door and called to me.

Giving Laddie's leash a gentle tug, I said, "Let's go see Belle."

We could hear Mr. Big barking inside the house.

"No crutches, I see."

"I'm done with them, but my ankle still bothers me. I suppose I'll be limping for a while, but it's easier than dragging those crutches around. I had Dennis return them to the drug store this morning."

"You're on the mend," I assured her. "That's the important thing."

Belle nodded. "I saw Dustin leaving a minute ago."

"I'll miss him. I suppose I'll have to make do with visits."

"It's hard. Both our sons still live in Michigan, but we see them fairly often. By the way, have you had a chance to look at the Bugle yet?" The Lonesome Valley Bugle was a newspaper delivered free to local residents once a week.

"Not yet. I was planning to read it after Dustin left."

"Well, why don't you and Laddie come in for a few minutes. I want to show you the Chamber of Commerce's ad."

"Sure."

Laddie and I trooped inside after Belle and were greeted by Mr. Big. Belle sat beside me on the sofa and opened the newspaper to the large center spread, an ad for the local Friday art studio tours, sponsored by the Chamber of Commerce. It included a large map with stars to mark each studio's location, along with a list of artists' studios and their addresses. The first thing I noticed was that my star was missing. There was no listing for my studio at all.

"I thought the Chamber promised to add you to the tour."

"They did," I said in dismay. "At least the lady I spoke with at the Chamber's office did. She said they were going to print new flyers with a new map to hand out and my studio would be included, starting next week. Looks like I'm out in the cold. I wonder what happened."

"Probably a bureaucratic snafu. Maybe they can correct it before they distribute the flyers."

"I hope so." I was afraid it was too late. "I should go check with them right away, but their office may not be open on Saturday."

"The Chamber's kiosk downtown should be open all weekend. Maybe whoever's staffing it can help."

"Good idea. I better find out right away. I'm glad you noticed it."

"Why don't you leave Laddie here with us. It looks as though their long walk this morning has them both tuckered out." Belle nodded toward Mr. Big's bed where he had curled up. Laddie lay on the floor next to him, his feet moving rapidly as though he were running.

"He's dreaming," I whispered as I quietly slipped out, without rousing the dogs.

Mona Lisa ignored me when I went home to grab my keys and purse before quickly exiting.

The Chamber of Commerce's kiosk, where greeters provided downtown visitors with brochures, maps, and other information, stood on the far end of Main Street. A large public parking lot next to the kiosk accommodated tourists and locals alike. Since the few parallel parking spaces along Main Street weren't adequate, the lot was a necessity to lure people to shop downtown. I found a space in the crowded lot and approached the kiosk, where a girl who appeared to be high-school age was handing some brochures to an older couple. As soon as they left, I stepped up to the counter. The girl wore a name badge. Lisa had long, brown hair, and, despite her eye make-up, now that I could see her up close, she looked even younger than I'd first thought.

"Hi, Lisa," I said. "I'm Amanda, and my art studio is supposed to be on the Friday night tour, but it wasn't listed on the map in today's Bugle."

Lisa looked confused for a moment. Then she grabbed a flyer from a shelf behind her and handed it to me.

"Is this what you're looking for?"

I scanned the map. Sure enough, my listing had been

omitted from the flyer, too. There was no star indicating my studio's location, either.

"This looks just like the map that was in the newspaper."

"Right. That's our new map."

"Well, how can I get it changed?"

"These are brand new. They were printed a couple of days ago. Maybe next time they're printed, you can get your studio listed."

"How often are they printed?"

"Oh, let me see. Usually about every three or four months, I guess."

I wanted to cry, but I wasn't ready to give up yet. Since it was obvious Lisa wasn't able to help me, I needed to find someone who could.

"Is anyone working at the Chamber's office today?" I asked her.

Lisa shrugged. "It's Saturday, so I doubt it."

"Maybe I'll check, anyway, just in case."

"Have a nice day," she said as I hurried off. Unfortunately, my day would be anything but nice if I missed out on the studio tour for the next three or four months. Like the Roadrunner Gallery, Lonesome Valley's Friday night tour of artists' studios had been a part of my plan to make my living as a full-time artist.

The Chamber of Commerce occupied a small, refurbished 1930s bungalow, a few blocks off Main Street. Rather than move my car, I walked. There was a closed sign on the front door, but through the filmy curtains, I could see that someone was inside, so I knocked. When there was no response, I tried again, knocking a little louder this time.

My efforts were rewarded when the door swung open, and I

was surprised to see Pamela, the gallery board member who'd wanted to become the Roadrunner's new director. We hadn't spoken since the day of my interview, and, from the blank look on her face when she opened the door and saw me, I wasn't sure that she remembered me.

"Hi, Pamela. I'm Amanda Trent from the gallery. I don't know if you remember me."

My reminder sparked a glimmer of recognition. "Oh, of course. Is there a problem at the gallery?"

"No. I'm here on another matter."

I was wondering if we were going to have our conversation standing in the doorway when she finally invited me to come in.

"I was just catching up on some paperwork. It's quiet here on Saturday. Have a seat."

Pamela sat down on a high-backed chair across from me in the reception area.

"I didn't realize you worked for the Chamber."

"Just part-time. I try to paint every morning, and I'm at the gallery, too, most days. I like to keep busy. My husband commutes to Phoenix for work, so I'm alone much of the time," she said wistfully. "Now, how can I help you, Amanda?" she asked, changing the subject.

I explained my dilemma, and Pamela said she'd track down the problem. Beckoning me to come with her, she went to a desk on the far side of the room, pulled a file out of the top drawer, and looked at the paperwork inside.

"Here's the problem: the printer didn't make the changes we requested, and since he didn't send us a proof to check, he's going to have to correct it and reprint our flyers on his dime. I'll get on this first thing Monday morning, and we should have the new flyers ready to hand out by Friday. I'll make sure our ad's corrected, too."

"I can't thank you enough, Pamela. I was afraid I wouldn't be listed for several months."

"It's important to be on the tour. Sometimes I get a bit discouraged when only a few people show up on Friday nights, but other times they come in droves. It's worth it then, especially when they buy my paintings or even if they just tell me they like my work. Oh, I almost forgot to check with you. Is your studio a separate building?"

"No. Is that required? It's attached to my house, but there's a separate, outside entrance to the studio."

"That's perfect. Even though everybody will have a map and a list of addresses, I find it helps to put a portable sign out by the curb on tour days."

"What a great idea! I'm not too handy, but I'll bet my neighbor can help me figure out how to make my sign."

Orchestral music suddenly started playing, and the cell phone lying on the desktop lit up. Chip's face appeared on the display, but Pamela grabbed the phone and quickly silenced it.

"Probably some gallery business. I'll call him back later," she muttered.

I wouldn't have thought anything about it, but Pamela seemed to feel she had to explain Chip's call to me, and that was odd.

"By the way, what do you think of Janice's sister as gallery director?" she asked.

"I guess time will tell," I said noncommittally.

"Frankly, I think the director should be someone who is already familiar with the gallery. Without Janice, the transition's going to be difficult enough, and Judith hasn't set foot in Lonesome Valley, let alone the gallery, for years, from what I understand."

The orchestral music sounded again, and Chip's face reappeared on Pamela's cell phone. She jabbed the phone hastily, and the display turned black.

"I should get going and give you a chance to finish your paperwork," I said. "Thank you so much for your help. I don't know what I would have done if the flyers couldn't be fixed."

"Glad to help, Amanda. I'll be seeing you at the gallery."

As I walked back to my car, I thought about Pamela's strange about-face. She'd been quite friendly and very helpful to me, the opposite of the way she'd acted during my interview. I reminded myself the same could be said of Chip and, to a lesser extent, Janice. I made a mental note to ask Susan if she knew why the committee members had been so aloof and uncommunicative during my interview. It didn't seem like a very good strategy to me. Even though I'd been accepted as a member of the gallery, I'd been almost paralyzed with anxiety before I received my official invitation to join in the mail the day after my interview. If there was any way to spare future potential members the same experience, I wanted to do it. Perhaps putting in my two cents about how the the interviews were conducted would convince the committee members to act differently next time.

The other thing I kept thinking about that struck me as strange was Pamela's dismissal of Chip's phone calls. If she was as worried about the gallery as she'd indicated, why wouldn't she have picked up his calls? On the other hand, maybe she hadn't wanted me to hear their conversation. I hoped she wasn't plotting to somehow take over as gallery director, despite Judith's election to the post.

Judith had already proven herself a formidable opponent, and I doubted she would change her mind. Like it or not, Judith ruled the Roadrunner, at least for the time being.

Chapter 15

I was in a good mood as I drove to the gallery Monday morning. Dustin had called me the night before to let me know that his trip back to Kansas City had gone off without a hitch. The judge and his wife were waiting for him when he arrived at their home. They'd shown Dustin where they wanted to put the painting in a dominant spot on the wall in their den, and Dustin had stayed long enough to help the power couple hang the landscape, before he'd texted me some photos of it in its place of honor. The delivery couldn't have gone more smoothly. My son had gone out of his way to make sure my first commissioned artwork arrived safely at its destination, and I felt very grateful. I knew I'd need to find a good art shipper, but next time, I'd add shipping charges to any out-of-town purchases.

When I reported for my shift at the gallery Monday morning, Judith opened the door for me promptly at nine o'clock. Susan had called me to say she was running late, so I passed the word on to Judith, who didn't look pleased.

She tasked me with dusting the gallery before retreating to the office formerly occupied by her sister and firmly closing the door.

My only customer for the first half hour was the owner of the gift shop across the street, who stopped in to purchase several note cards. Monday morning was bound to be a slow time, and I reconciled myself to watching the clock until my four-hour shift ended at one.

The minutes dragged slowly by. Susan still hadn't shown up by ten, but Judith hadn't emerged from the office, so she didn't realize how late my mentor was.

I was stifling a yawn when I saw Ralph, the elderly man who'd sat next to me at the meeting, coming toward the gallery, carrying a large painting. I rushed to hold the door open for him as he juggled the painting.

"Thanks," he said as he came in and set the painting down carefully, leaning it against the wall under his other paintings. "You're the new member, aren't you?"

"Yes."

He snapped his fingers as though he'd remembered something. "You were sitting next to me at our meeting. Amanda, right?"

"That's right. I was here last week when your fabulous painting sold. This must be its replacement," I said, taking a closer look at the work. I couldn't help noticing its beautiful, but undoubtedly expensive, frame, too.

"Lovely landscape," I said.

"In a fabulous frame," Judith added, coming up behind me. I hadn't heard her approach, and I jumped.

"I didn't mean to startle you, Amanda," she said.

"Sorry. I didn't hear you." What I didn't say was that had she been wearing the stilettos she'd worn when she opened the gallery door for me, I definitely would have heard a staccato click-click-click on the hardwood floor. I couldn't help looking at her feet. She wore the same type of crepe-soled shoes that Janice had worn each time I'd seen her.

Judith saw me staring at her shoes. She looked a bit embarrassed. "I'm afraid the high heels might damage the floor," she explained. "I borrowed some of Janice's shoes." I had the feeling Judith's switching shoes had more to do with comfort than a concern for the floor. After all, customers wore all kinds of footwear when they came into the gallery. I couldn't really blame her, though. I didn't know how women who were on their feet all day managed in sky-high heels. I thought of Brooks Miller's wife and her pricey Louboutins. After standing all day in her husband's gallery, her feet must be killing her.

Judith and I watched as Ralph re-arranged the display of his paintings. Finally, he lifted his newest work into its place on the wall and stepped back to make sure it was positioned perfectly.

"Wonderful!" Judith exclaimed. "Another winner. Your work is always so . . . ," she trailed off, seeming to forget what she'd intended to say. Suddenly, she turned to me, "Where's Susan? She should have been here over an hour ago."

"I don't know. She told me she was running late but didn't say why. Would you like me to call her?"

"Yes. We're supposed to have two members staffing the gallery at all times, and I can't stay on the floor all morning. I have an appointment."

"I can stay if Susan isn't able to make it this morning," Ralph volunteered. "I'd just be puttering around at home, anyway."

"If you don't mind," Judith said.

"Sure. Not a problem."

"All right then. I'll be in the office. I'm expecting Lieutenant

Belmont. Please tap on the door when he gets here."

The detective was the last person in the world I wanted to see. If I spotted him on his way into the gallery, I'd definitely hide in the restroom and let Ralph take him to see Judith.

After Judith returned to the office, I decided to let Ralph in on my strategy and my reason for wanting to avoid the lieutenant. Ralph nodded in an absent-minded way when I told him my story, but he agreed to cover for me.

I noticed that he was rubbing his gnarled hands together and wincing in pain. I surmised that was probably the reason he hadn't appeared to be paying close attention to what I'd told him.

"Arthritis is kicking up again," he said. "Some days it's so bad I can't paint. Just can't get a good grip on my brushes. I do what I can on the good days."

"From the looks of it, that's quite a lot," I said, pointing to his latest painting.

Mindful of the possible arrival of the detective at any moment, I looked out the front gallery window every few minutes. Ralph and I were discussing home remedies for arthritis pain when I spotted the detective getting out of his car across the street. Luckily, he didn't see me, and I headed to the restroom after I clued Ralph in.

I felt foolish hiding from the lieutenant, but there was no need to borrow trouble. He hadn't tried to contact me since I'd walked out of the police station, but if he saw me, he might decide to question me again, so avoiding him seemed to be my best course of action.

Listening at the door of the restroom, I could hear voices. I didn't want to come out until the detective went into the office for his appointment with Judith, so I stayed put until there was silence before peeking out. I looked around and didn't see anyone except Ralph, so I joined him.

After Ralph assured me the coast was clear for now, he said, "We might as well take a load off. I doubt that we have more than a handful of customers this morning."

"It's not busy; that's for sure. I think I'll give Susan a call. I hope she didn't have car trouble."

Susan didn't answer my call, so I left a message for her. I hadn't gotten the impression that anything was wrong when I'd talked to her earlier. She'd sounded like she was hurrying to get ready, instead. I realized that had been hours ago, though, and I was starting to worry.

"No luck?" Ralph asked.

I shook my head.

Ralph frowned. "It's not like Susan to be late. We were on the board together for several years, and she was always punctual. Never missed a meeting, either."

"Maybe she'll call me back. If not and she doesn't show up by one, I think I'll go by her house to check on her. Maybe she's not feeling well."

Lieutenant Belmont had been in the office with Judith for only a few minutes, so I didn't expect their meeting to end so soon, but when Ralph and I heard the office door open, I scurried back to hide in the restroom again while the detective took his leave.

When I came out, Ralph and Judith were standing next to the counter. When I joined them, I was in for a shock.

"I found out why Susan isn't here this morning," Ralph said.

"Is she OK?" I asked. The somber look on Ralph's face seemed to indicate otherwise.

"She's in jail," Judith said. "Susan's been arrested for murdering my sister."

"What? That can't be right! Susan and I came into the gallery together that morning, and we were together when we found Janice. This doesn't make any sense."

"The lieutenant wouldn't give me any details." Judith said. "I must say it's hard to believe, though."

"But what possible reason could Susan have had for killing Janice? She had good things to say about her, even though she admitted they didn't always agree."

A shadow crossed Judith's face. "You really think the police arrested the wrong person, don't you?"

"I certainly do. I can't imagine that Susan had any motive at all. She doesn't strike me as a dangerous person."

"I agree. I think the police have it all wrong," Ralph chimed in. "I hope Susan has a good lawyer. Somebody sure needs to get to the bottom of this and find the real killer. If the police think they already have the right person in custody, they're not likely to look any further."

Judith shuddered. "If you're right, that means whoever killed Janice is still on the loose."

Chapter 16

I felt sick. Granted I hadn't known Susan for very long, but I couldn't believe she was a killer.

Judith looked shaken by the news, too. "I'll be in my office," she said tersely, leaving Ralph and me to speculate about the bombshell she'd dropped.

"Mrs. Trent!" There was no mistaking the source of *that* bellow. It could only be Lieutenant Belmont, who'd come back into the gallery while Ralph and I were discussing the shocking turn of events. There was no place to hide now that he'd already seen me. I turned to face the detective.

"We didn't finish our interview the other day. I have a few questions for you, and I'd advise you to answer them. If you don't cooperate, you can expect a subpoena from the district attorney when our case goes to court."

"I can't leave now," I hedged, unwilling to be trapped in the interview room at the police station again.

"All right. We'll do it right here, right now. There's no time like the present."

Ralph didn't need any encouragement from the lieutenant to leave us alone. He drifted into the back area of the gallery, out of earshot.

"When did you first see Ms. Carpenter the day of the murder?"

"I already told you. We met outside the gallery a few minutes before nine o'clock."

"Who found the body?"

"I already told you that, too. We were together when we discovered Janice lying on the floor."

"Did Ms. Carpenter mention coming to the gallery earlier that morning?"

"No."

"Did you get here first or was she waiting for you when you arrived?"

"Umm. Let's see," I said, trying to remember. "She was here first."

I didn't really want to answer that question because it could look bad for Susan, but I felt I had no choice. Like he said, the district attorney could issue a subpoena for me to testify at trial. I could see where he was going with his interrogation. His theory must be that Susan showed up at the gallery earlier than I did and killed Janice before I arrived. I wished I could have provided a more concrete alibi for her, but I didn't know of anything else I could say that would help her. The bottom line was I really didn't know much at all.

"We're done here—for now. I may have more questions later, and I expect you to make yourself available," he said before he left the gallery for the second time.

I was so shaken by the news of Susan's arrest and my run-in with the lieutenant that I didn't pay much attention as a few potential customers visited the gallery and Ralph rang up a small sale. I felt as though I should be doing something to help Susan, but I was afraid that my answers to the detective's questions had had the opposite effect.

As distracted as I felt, I was relieved when my morning shift ended. When Lonnie and his wife Heather arrived for the afternoon, I introduced myself. Before we had a chance to chat, Judith came out of her office and told the couple she needed to confirm the arrangements for the children's art classes they were scheduled to teach. Ralph and I weren't involved in the classes, so we said our good-byes.

I planned on making a quick stop at the supermarket on the way home. Monday afternoon wasn't a busy time for shoppers, and I quickly found what I needed, went through the self-checkout line, wheeled my shopping cart to my car, and popped open the trunk.

"She walks in beauty."

Startled, I turned and saw Chip coming toward me with a big grin on his face.

"Chip!"

"Let me get those for you," he said and began loading my bags into the trunk before I could open my mouth to protest.

For a man whose aunt had just been arrested for murder, he seemed awfully cheerful. Then it dawned on me that he probably hadn't heard the bad news yet.

"Chip, there's something I have to tell you."

"You're ready to have that dinner with me now," he guessed.

"No. That's not it."

"But I'd really like to get to know you better."

"Chip, this is important. Please listen to me," I said, ignoring his flirtatious comment.

"I'm all ears."

"Susan's been arrested for murdering Janice!"

Chip's demeanor changed immediately. "Aunt Susan? I don't believe it."

"I'm sorry, but it's true. Lieutenant Belmont came to the gallery this morning to inform Judith."

"No way did Aunt Susan kill anyone. You don't believe she did it, do you?"

"Of course not. I was with her when we found Janice, remember? She was as shocked as I was."

"Dad hasn't called me. He must not have heard about it yet, either. We have to do something. Convince that jerk of a cop that she didn't kill Janice."

"He's made up his mind, and he's not an easy man to talk to."

Chip frowned. "I remember. When he questioned me, he implied that I'd killed Janice, and I wasn't even in town that day."

"She'll need a lawyer," I suggested. "I don't see how the police can have any hard evidence against her. I think their case is entirely circumstantial supposition."

"Right. She needs a lawyer," he repeated. "I'd better give Dad the bad news that the cops think his baby sister's a killer. This is crazy! See you later, Amanda. I'll keep you posted," he promised as he jumped into his car.

Although telling Chip about Susan's arrest made me feel unsettled, it had certainly put an end to his flirtatious behavior. With my mind on Susan's plight, rather than on trying to discourage him, I feared I'd left the door open to another advance. Right now, he was focused on his aunt, but he'd promised to keep me posted, and, curious as I was to find out what was going on, I hadn't told him not to. I knew I'd have to deal with him later, but I would have preferred to avoid it. When I'd told Dustin that I wasn't interested in dating, I'd meant it.

When I arrived home with the groceries, Laddie ran to me and stayed by my side while I put them away, but Mona Lisa, displaying her enigmatic look, played coy and watched us from the top of her kitty perch. She didn't move when Laddie and I went to the backyard to play fetch, and she remained in the same position until we came back inside. When she saw us, she leaped down and scooted off to the bedroom where she hid under the bed. I often wondered what went on in her kitty mind and what caused her to be loving or playful one moment and aloof or withdrawn the next. Unlike Laddie, whose moves and temperament were reliably golden, Mona Lisa remained a bit of a mystery, and I suspected she liked it that way.

I skipped lunch and spent the rest of the afternoon in the studio, painting, while Laddie kept me company. I played some soothing music, and he curled up and took a long nap. It was beginning to get dark when I called a halt for the day. I wiped my brushes to remove as much paint as possible and then dipped their tips in safflower oil before putting them on a drying rack. I had quite a bit of paint left on my palette, so I set it, paint and all, into the freezer to keep since I loved the colors I'd mixed and planned to use them again in the morning.

I didn't often miss a meal, so I was too hungry to spend a lot of time preparing dinner. I dished out a large helping of leftover taco casserole and put it in the microwave to heat. While I waited, I filled my pets' bowls. I didn't need to call them to dinner. They were both at my heels as I set their bowls on their personalized placemats on opposite sides of the kitchen. Although Laddie had never bothered Mona Lisa while she was eating, I couldn't say the same for the finicky feline. She'd been known to take a swipe at Laddie if he so much as ventured too close to her bowl, so I'd learned to keep them separated to maintain peace.

I added a generous dollop of my homemade guacamole to my plate, along with some shredded lettuce, grape tomatoes, and corn chips before putting my dinner on a tray. I plunked down in my recliner, pointed my remote at the television, and found a new movie I wanted to watch. After standing all day, it felt good to put my feet up. Laddie lay quietly beside me, but I had to fend off Mona Lisa temporarily so that I could eat. As soon as I finished my dinner, I put my tray aside and invited Mona Lisa to join me. She curled up on my lap, purring loudly, and I stroked her soft fur while I watched the movie.

An hour and a half later when the movie ended, Mona Lisa was still on my lap. When I got up to take my dishes to the kitchen, I gently settled her on the wide arm of the chair, but she leaped down as Laddie jumped up, and they both followed me to the kitchen.

After I loaded my few dishes into the dishwasher, I gave Mona Lisa a kitty treat and Laddie a chewy. I munched on the last peanut butter cookie left from the plateful that Belle had given Dustin. Somehow, Dustin had forgotten the lone cookie left from the batch, or perhaps he'd saved it for me since he'd eaten most of the others.

A light, rhythmic tap sounded on the side door to the carport. I recognized it immediately as Belle's signal. Laddie knew her unique knock, too, and he beat me to the door. Both Belle and Dennis stood outside, in my carport.

Chapter 17

"I have something to show you," Dennis said.

"Come in," I invited them.

"Why don't you come out here? It's kind of bulky," Belle giggled.

I switched on the light in the carport and stepped out, Laddie at my heels. Belle and Dennis moved aside, revealing what they'd been hiding. It was a sign for my art studio.

"Oh, that's perfect!" I exclaimed, examining it closely. The sturdy wooden sign, hinged at the top, had a chain attached at the bottom connecting the two boards so that the sign would stand up. What really caught my eye, though, were the graphics. Emblazoned on each side were the words, "Amanda Trent Art Studio," in a calligraphy-like script over a printed background of one of my landscapes.

Dennis surprised me by sliding out one of the signs from its wooden frame. "You can change these any time. See," he said pointing to grooves in the wood. "You can remove your graphic from either side and replace it with a different one. You just slide it in, and these slats will hold it in place. Oh, also, I had them laminated. That'll give them some protection in case it's raining on a studio tour day."

"Awesome! I'm overwhelmed. It looks so beautiful. Where did you find the picture?"

"Remember when you couldn't find your digital camera right after you moved in, and I took some pictures with mine so you could update your website? I still have them on my camera, too," Belle said.

"Of course. That seems like ages ago, but it's only been a few months. I can't thank you both enough. When I mentioned it to you, I thought you were going to help me figure out how to make it. I didn't realize you were going to do all the work yourselves."

"We figured you had enough on your plate, and, besides, when it comes to building anything, Dennis is a master. When we moved here, he tore out all the old kitchen cabinets and built new ones."

"I didn't know that. You're very talented," I told him.

"Thanks, Amanda." He smiled. "Now there's one more thing. This sign is kind of heavy, so I rigged up a little trolley that you can use when you set it out for your studio tours. This way, you can wheel it out to the curb, rather than carrying it. You'll have to lift it on and off the trolley, but I made it as low as I could."

"Another genius idea! You've thought of everything."

"Don't forget the arrows, Dennis," Belle reminded him.

"Oh, right. To make the directions crystal clear for your customers, I made a couple of arrow signs. They each fit into a metal rod I've already installed next to your sidewalk. Don't worry, the rods are flush with the ground, so nobody will trip over them. I installed some solar lights along the sidewalk, too."

"I never noticed. When did you have time to do all this?"

"I took the morning off, so I could get everything done

while you worked at the gallery."

"We wanted to surprise you," Belle said.

"You certainly did. Let me pay you for the supplies. I know all this couldn't have been cheap."

"Well, you're right about that. It's going to cost you."

"Dennis!" Belle sounded exasperated as she poked him in the arm. "Don't give Amanda a hard time."

"It's going to cost you one of those chocolate meringue pies you make—or three," Dennis chuckled.

"Done!" I agreed. "I'll throw in a couple of my apricot cream pies, too."

"It's a deal," Dennis said. "Do you want to store the sign in your studio? It'll make your trip to the curb a lot shorter."

I nodded. "Good idea."

"We'll go through the house so Amanda can unlock the studio door and meet you there," Belle told Dennis. "I don't want to stumble around in the dark. One sprained ankle's about all I can handle."

Laddie trotted along with us as we went through my small abode and into the studio. When I opened the outside door for Dennis, we could hear him coming before we saw him since the rollers on the trolley sounded a bit like a skateboard on the cement sidewalk. I hastily cleared a spot in the corner next to the door.

"Right here would be good," I said, and Dennis parked the trolley with my new sign atop it.

"Amanda, it's still fairly dark out there, even with the solar lights I installed. I think motion lights would help quite a bit. It wouldn't hurt to have three others, too. Cover the carport and the front and backyard."

"Sounds expensive."

"It could be, what with an electrician's charge for labor. I have a battery-operated spotlight you could use, instead. I can adjust it to throw more light on the sidewalk to the studio, at least. Of course, it won't do anything for the rest of the yard, but your customers only need to locate the studio anyway, and your sign will be right under the street light, so they shouldn't have a bit of trouble finding you."

"That would be great, Dennis. I may have to throw in a few of my pecan pies, too."

"I love those!" Belle said enthusiastically. "They're so sweet it's just like eating candy, and you know what a sweet tooth Dennis and I both have."

Laddie's ears perked up, but it wasn't because Belle mentioned pie. He'd heard a noise, and he ran to the outside studio door, which we'd left ajar.

"Knock. Knock. I saw the lights were on," Chip said, rapping on the door frame. "How are you doing, fella?" He stooped to pat Laddie on the head.

Belle must have recognized Chip as the pizza delivery man who'd brought us our lunch the day she'd sprained her ankle because she turned to me and asked me whether I'd ordered a pizza.

"No. Chip's a board member of the gallery."

"And I deliver pizza, too. My dad owns a pizza parlor," he explained, shaking hands with Belle and Dennis as I made the introductions.

"Well, we'd best be on our way," Dennis said. He probably thought Chip and I had gallery business to take care of.

"Don't go. Belle and I were about to set up her new website, and we need your feedback," I fibbed, desperately hoping that Belle would play along. I shot her a pleading look. Although I hadn't mentioned Chip and his previous flirtatious behavior to Belle, she picked up on what I was trying to tell her right away: I did not want to be left alone with Chip.

At first Dennis looked confused when Belle confirmed that we did indeed want him to give us his opinion about Belle's nonexistent new website, but then he seemed to pick up Belle's vibe and went along with the program, leaving Chip the odd man out.

"You're a busy lady, Amanda," Chip said. "It seems like every time I see you, you're in the middle of something."

"There's a lot going on," I said.

"I won't keep you, but I wanted to let you know that Dad was able to talk to Aunt Susan at the station for a few minutes before they transferred her to the jail."

Belle gasped, and Dennis looked shocked.

"Your mentor, Susan?" Belle asked me.

I nodded.

Chip jumped in. "It's all right to tell them, Amanda. We found out the police put out a press release that they'd arrested Janice's killer. That'll make the eleven o'clock news for sure, and it'll be in the morning paper. By tomorrow, everyone in town will know. It's not right. Aunt Susan wouldn't hurt a fly."

"Not only that, but she had no motive. She spoke well of Janice even though she said they'd had some disagreements in the past. Poor Susan! I can't imagine her having to suffer in jail. Isn't there supposed to be some kind of a bail hearing?" I asked.

"Tomorrow morning, she's scheduled for what they call an initial appearance in court. That's when the judge might release her if she posts a bond, but since they're charging her with homicide, the judge may not grant bail."

"I hope she has a good lawyer if Belmont's made up his

mind that she's guilty. He's tenacious," Dennis said.

"Sounds like you know him."

"Unfortunately, I do. Hard to find a more pig-headed man."

"I got that impression, too, when he questioned me. He's interviewed every single member of the gallery. There are plenty of other members who've argued with Janice. I can't understand why he focused on Aunt Susan. Anyway, Amanda, I wanted to ask you if you could come with me to court tomorrow. You know, to offer Aunt Susan moral support?"

"Umm. Sure. OK."

"Her appearance is scheduled for ten. Pick you up about nine-thirty?"

"Oh, no," I said hastily. "I have errands to run in the morning. I'll meet you at the courthouse."

"Well, all right. I'll see you there tomorrow."

Although I knew Chip was genuinely concerned about Susan, he evidently also saw Susan's court appearance as yet another opportunity to connect with me. I definitely needed to have a talk with him, but now wasn't the appropriate time.

After Chip left, closing the studio's outside door behind him, Dennis turned to Belle. "You didn't tell me you were setting up a website."

Belle and I looked at each other and burst into giggles.

"What gives, ladies?"

"I'm sorry, Dennis. I'm afraid the website doesn't exist. I was trying to think of some reason to keep you and Belle here because I didn't want to be alone with Chip. He showed up out of the blue in the evening once before, but Dustin was here at the time, so he didn't hang around. Dustin's convinced that Chip wants to date me, even though I'm old enough to be his mother. I know it seems crazy. I'd like to avoid him, but that could be difficult since we're both members of the gallery, and his aunt is my mentor."

"No wonder you didn't want him to pick you up tomorrow," Belle said.

"It's unfortunate about his aunt, but I don't like the idea of him showing up uninvited here at night," Dennis said. "If he does it again, give us a call, and we'll pay you a neighborly visit."

"I'll definitely do that. I think he's probably harmless, but . . . ."

"You never know," Belle said, finishing my thought.

Chapter 18

The more I thought about it, the more I felt freaked out by Chip's second sudden appearance at my home. I wanted to get along with him, but only as a colleague at the gallery, not as a romantic interest, and I didn't appreciate having my privacy invaded. I resolved to tell him so in no uncertain terms at the first possible opportunity, before the situation became untenable. Hopefully, he'd listen to reason and back off.

When I arrived at the courthouse the next morning, Chip was nowhere to be found. He hadn't told me where Susan's appearance was scheduled, only the time—ten o'clock. I looked around to see if I could find any information. People were purposefully bustling about, all evidently headed toward a known destination. When I saw a man come out of one of the courtrooms wearing a badge identifying him as a bailiff, I decided to ask him for directions. He told me that he wasn't familiar with the case, but that he would check for me. The bailiff was back a few minutes later with news.

"There's nothing listed with Susan Carpenter's name on the docket today," he told me.

"What does that mean? Has her appearance been rescheduled?"

"I'm sorry. That's the only information I have."

"Thank you for checking."

I returned to my car, wondering what had happened. Since Chip wasn't at the courthouse to meet me, I surmised that he knew the answer, but I wasn't about to call him to find out. I didn't have his phone number, anyway, but I knew he must have mine. After all, he'd found my address by looking me up in the Roadrunner's member directory, which also listed members' phone numbers, email addresses, and websites.

I'd just put my key into the ignition when my smartphone rang. Chip must be calling, I thought, but when I dug my phone out of my bag, Susan's smiling face filled the display. I'd taken her picture the first day we'd met, when she came to the studio to see my artwork and clue me in about my gallery membership.

"Susan, are you OK?"

"I'm out of jail, but I'm not exactly OK. The last twenty-four hours have been the worst of my life—being arrested by that awful Lieutenant Belmont and then spending a sleepless night in jail. I can't begin to describe how bad it was."

"I'm so sorry."

"I'm out now, so you'd think I'd feel relieved but not so much because, right before they let me go, Belmont told me he planned to keep tabs on me, and as soon as he gathers more evidence, he's going to arrest me again. I want to warn you, Amanda, that he kept implying that you were covering for me. He's convinced himself that I was already inside the gallery when you got there the morning Janice was killed."

"But that's ridiculous! I told him we met in front of the gallery."

"I know," Susan sounded very weary. There was a catch in her throat when she said, "I wanted to give you a heads-up. The man's relentless. He questioned me for hours before my attorney showed up and put a stop to it. By then, I'd repeated the same story over and over. It seemed like a hundred times. I wish I hadn't said anything at all. If my brother hadn't hired a lawyer, I don't know what I would have done."

"Oh, Susan, how awful! How were you able to be released? Did you have to post a bond? Chip told me you had to make an initial appearance in court this morning."

"My nephew's another story, but my lawyer talked to the district attorney, who agreed not to pursue the case now, due to lack of evidence, but he said they could file charges if the police investigation uncovers more evidence. I don't know how there can be any evidence because I haven't done anything wrong."

"If only the police could find the real killer," I said.

"Yeah, like that's going to happen. They're not even looking at anybody else except me. Amanda, I'm exhausted. I'm going to take a hot shower, pop some melatonin, and go to bed. I didn't sleep a wink last night. I do want to talk with you about Chip, though. I'm too tired to think straight right at the moment. Let me call you when I wake up, if that's all right."

"Sure. That's fine. Get some rest."

I was curious about what Susan wanted to tell me about Chip, but it would have to wait. I wondered if it had anything to do with his failure to meet me at the courthouse, but I felt relieved to have avoided seeing him there, rather than angry that he hadn't shown up.

Although I was glad that Susan had been released from jail, it was nerve-wracking that the lieutenant remained so single-minded in his belief that she'd killed Janice. I was more than a little concerned that he thought I was covering for her, especially considering that I'd told him everything I knew. I reminded myself that I wasn't compelled to talk to him, and I resolved not to answer any more of his questions in the future. If he kept insisting on going off on the wrong track, he could go there without me.

I hadn't started my car yet when I received a text message from Pamela, inviting me to double check the proof of the new flyer for the Friday night studio tours. She'd had it delivered to her at home, rather than to the Chamber's office because she'd be working in her own studio all day. When I replied in the affirmative, she texted me her address, along with directions, and said to come anytime, so I decided to stop by Pamela's studio before going home.

Pamela's lovely and very large home stood at the end of a cul-de-sac in an upscale neighborhood. Like her neighbors' homes, Pamela's featured Southwest styling, paint in earth-tone colors, a red tile roof, and desert landscaping. I pulled into the semicircular driveway, paved with bricks in the same soft red hue as the roof, and parked behind a white Nissan. According to Pamela's directions, I should follow the sidewalk around the house and through a gate to her studio in the back. Her directions were easy to follow, but I wondered how she directed her studio tour guests to the right spot. I wouldn't have known there was a separate studio on the property if Pamela hadn't told me. I walked past a patio, swimming pool, and pool house. The grounds looked very inviting, planted with desert bushes, and the sidewalk was lined with pots of colorful blooming plants. When I went around the pool house to find the studio, I guessed that the stand-alone building had originally been intended as a guesthouse and that Pamela had converted it into her art studio.

I was several yards away from the studio when the door opened, and Chip emerged, followed by Pamela. They hadn't seen me, and I had no desire to talk to Chip, so I jumped behind a huge, leafy bush next to the sidewalk. It was large enough to conceal my presence, and I hoped Chip would walk right past me, without realizing I was there.

I didn't think he would notice me as long as I stood very still and didn't make any noise. I stayed frozen there for a while, but Chip didn't come by, so I cautiously parted the leaves that blocked my view of Pamela's studio. Chip hadn't left yet. He was kissing Pamela, and his kiss was no mere peck on the cheek, either. Pamela wasn't resisting in the slightest. When their lips finally parted, she clung to him for a few seconds before letting go. She didn't stay outside to watch him leave, but returned to her studio, closing the door behind her.

Whistling, Chip came down the walk toward me. I moved a few steps to one side so that the bush blocked his view of me as he passed by. Although I felt confident he hadn't seen me, I stayed where I was for several minutes. The car I'd parked behind must be Chip's, I thought, wondering whether he'd notice my own car in the driveway when he left and whether he'd realize who owned it.

I lingered outside for about ten more minutes before I approached the door to the studio. I rang the doorbell, and Pamela answered through an intercom.

"Come in, Amanda. The door's open."

There must have been a camera there, but it was so well concealed, I didn't notice it.

Light and airy, Pamela's studio occupied the great room of the former guesthouse. Pamela offered a quick tour, and I followed her as she showed me the kitchenette, office, bedroom, and bathroom. The place would have been a perfect guesthouse. Now, it was a perfect art studio.

I tried to put the image of that lingering kiss out of my mind as Pamela showed me around. Her colorful acrylic paintings of tropical scenes and exotic animals were professionally displayed on the walls. Only one half-finished painting stood on an easel next to a table where Pamela kept her art supplies.

The exuberance and the vibrant hues of Pamela's paintings provided a sharp counterpoint to her own persona, so much so that it was difficult to believe that the artist who'd painted them and Pamela, who'd dressed in shades of drab brown and tan every time I'd seen her, could be the same person.

"Would you like some coffee, Amanda? I just brewed a fresh pot."

"Sure. That sounds good."

"Have a seat," she invited, setting a china teacup on the table in the alcove that jutted off the kitchenette. She poured me coffee and set the pot on a trivet in front of me while she retrieved a sugar bowl and creamer and set them next to the coffee pot.

"I'll grab the proof. I left it in the office."

She returned in a minute and handed me the document.

"It looks right to me, but since we had a problem with it before, I want to make sure," Pamela said.

"It's fine," I said, looking at the proof. The star marking my studio's location was right where it should be, and my address was correct, too.

"Good. I'll let the printer know we approved it. We should have the new flyers by Friday, and I've corrected our newspaper ad, too. I'll recycle the old flyers so they won't be distributed by mistake."

"Thank you, Pamela. I really appreciate all your help."

Although I'd felt uneasy about seeing Pamela after witnessing the scene between her and Chip, I forced myself to keep my mind on our art connections. Even though Pamela had talent and money, she must be lonely, and I guessed that, since both Pamela and Chip were on the Roadrunner's board, he'd learned about the void in her life from Pamela herself and had taken the opportunity to fill it.

Thinking about their connection as board members reminded me of the first time I'd seen both of them at my membership interview. Ever since that distressing day, I'd wondered why the committee—Janice, Pamela, and Chip—had acted in such a cold way toward me. Maybe she wouldn't tell me, but I thought now might be a good time to broach the subject with Pamela.

"Pamela, you've been such a great help getting this flyer situation straightened out." I took a deep breath. "I wonder if I could ask another favor."

"Ask away," she said as she poured herself a cup of coffee and stirred in two liberal spoonfuls of sugar.

"OK. This may not be any of my business, but I wanted to ask you about my membership interview."

"Oh, that." Pamela looked embarrassed. "I guess I was hoping you wouldn't ask. Chip and I never should have gone along with Janice."

Clearly, Pamela knew exactly what I meant.

"So it was Janice's idea to give me the cold shoulder?"

Pamela nodded. "Not you, in particular, but anyone who applied for membership."

"Why would she want to do that?" I asked. "When I left the gallery that day, I thought you were going to reject my application."

"I'm sorry about that. Like I said, we never should have agreed to play it Janice's way, but she had such a strong will, it was hard to contradict her. Somehow, she always managed to get her own way."

"I still don't understand."

"It all started after we interviewed another artist a couple of months ago. We rejected her application, and there were some repercussions. Chip and I wanted to accept her, but Janice didn't. We finally gave in to her because we realized that if we accepted her application, Janice would do everything in her considerable power to see that the woman resigned, so we ended up going along with Janice's wishes.

"The artist didn't take the rejection well, and she came into the gallery several times to find out why we hadn't accepted her as a member. Janice managed to avoid her at first, but when she finally did speak with her, she said the decision of the committee was final and refused to discuss it. The poor lady left in tears. I felt terrible because I knew she had expected to be invited to join. Chip and I had been friendly with her and had praised her sculptures during the interview. After that incident, Janice insisted that we give absolutely no encouragement whatsoever to prospective members during their interviews."

"You certainly succeeded. I was so sure that you planned to turn me down that I almost fainted when I received my acceptance letter the next day. What did Janice find so objectionable about the artist's work?"

"She said it was craft, not art, and she also thought it was too whimsical and not particularly salable. The lady makes needle-felted animals from wool roving. I was fascinated with her sculptures myself, and there's no doubt in my mind that they're art. Janice may have had a point about possible sales, though. I don't really know how popular they would have been. Unfortunately, Janice never considered any work a proper sculpture unless it was made of metal or stone. That's why she and Susan had such go-rounds about Susan's papier mâché animal sculptures."

"How did Susan manage to convince Janice to let her display them?"

"She didn't, really. Susan was already a gallery member who was selling lots of watercolors when she added papier mâché sculptures to her repertoire. Even though our by-laws state that the gallery director must approve artwork on display, they also provide an exception if a majority of the board approves. It's the one and only time since I've been a member of the board that Janice was overruled on anything. Once she found out how popular Susan's animals were, she relented a bit."

"So when Susan told me she and Janice had had disagreements in the past, that's what she must have meant."

"I assume so."

"Could that be the reason the police suspect her of murdering Janice? It seems awfully thin to me. Surely Susan wasn't the only member who ever had a disagreement with Janice."

"No, she wasn't, but Susan's the only member who ever threatened to kill her."

Chapter 19

"What? That's hard to believe."

"I heard her. She was very angry, but I'm sure she didn't mean it. Her exact words were, 'I could kill that woman.' Susan and Janice were arguing in Janice's office, but the door wasn't closed, and they were both loud. When Susan left Janice's office, she slammed the door closed. That's when she said it. Several members were in the gallery at the time, and we all heard her. Like I said, I'm sure she didn't mean it literally. She was just blowing off steam. Unfortunately, when the police asked me whether I knew of any threats against Janice, I felt I had to report it. I know other members did the same."

"I suppose that could have prompted Lieutenant Belmont to take a closer look at Susan, but it seems awfully weak to me. After all, they'd evidently patched up their differences. There must be something more," I speculated.

Pamela shrugged. "Honestly, I have no idea what it could be. Despite what she said, I don't believe Susan's capable of such violence."

We chatted a while longer, the subject turning back to the Friday night art tours. By the time I left Pamela's studio, I had all but forgotten about the passionate kiss I'd observed, but when I passed the bush I'd hidden behind earlier, I was reminded. I wondered again whether Chip had noticed my car in the driveway when he left. If he had and if he realized the car belonged to me, I wondered whether or not he'd stop flirting with me since he would know I'd seen him and Pamela together.

Although I didn't want to date Chip, I didn't dislike him, but I couldn't help thinking of him in the same way as I thought of my son's friends. If I knew him better, I'd give him the same warning I'd given Dustin when he'd planned to go ahead with his date after he'd learned the beautiful manager of the Brooks Miller Gallery was married. Since I didn't know Chip well enough to tell him that he was playing with fire, I didn't plan to bring up the subject.

Knowing Laddie and Mona Lisa would be eagerly awaiting their mid-day treat, I headed for home and a warm welcome from both my pets. I took my paints out of the freezer and set them in the studio. By the time I'd eaten lunch and played fetch with Laddie, they'd be ready to use.

During the afternoon, I thought of Susan's dilemma as I worked on my latest landscape. By late afternoon, when I stopped work for the day, she hadn't yet called me. I assumed she was still sleeping, and I decided that she might enjoy having some comfort food for her dinner. She could probably use some pampering right now, but since she lived alone, there was nobody at home to pamper her.

I filled two large ceramic casserole dishes with my mac and cheese, topped with buttered bread crumbs. I mixed batter for a chocolate cake, poured it into two steel springform pans, and popped them into the oven when I removed the mac and cheese. My tiny oven was made to fit into my tiny kitchen, and it didn't work well to jam several pans into it at once. I planned on keeping one dish of mac and cheese and taking the other to Susan, along with the chocolate cake.

After I baked and cooled the cake, I iced one layer with a thick, creamy fudge frosting before carefully setting the top layer on it and finishing the frosting. I didn't know whether Susan was a chocaholic or not, but if she was, she'd like my cake, and, if not, I'd make her a different dessert tomorrow.

She called as I ran my knife through the icing to make a final swirl.

"Tell me you've been sleeping all this time," I said. "I know how tired you were."

"I have. It was heavenly to sleep in my own bed with my own pillows. They don't give you a pillow at the jail, not that I could sleep there, anyway."

"It sounds horrible."

"Believe me, it was. It's hard, but I'm going to try to put it out of my mind for the rest of the evening. I'd still like to talk to you about Chip. Would you be able to come over for dinner? We can order from Miguel's, if you like. They deliver."

"I have a better idea. I just finished making you mac and cheese and a chocolate cake. I can be there in a few minutes."

"Sounds delicious. I'm starting to feel hungry again. I haven't had a bite to eat since yesterday."

"In that case, I'd better hurry. I'll be there soon."

I heated Susan's mac and cheese, then stowed it in an insulated casserole carrier before placing the cake in its own plastic carrier. Both had handles, which made transporting them easier as I loaded them into my car.

Maybe I imagined it, but my pets looked a little sad when I left them home alone for the second time that day. The upside wouldn't come until I returned, and we'd have a happy reunion.

Susan had already set out placemats, plates, and silverware for us on her dining room table. The mac and cheese was still warm, so we didn't re-heat it.

"Umm. This is just what I needed. I guess that's why they call it comfort food," Susan said, taking a second helping. "And it's delicious, by the way."

"Glad you like it. I hope you're a chocolate lover," I said, removing the lid of the cake carrier.

"My favorite, and I'm going to have a huge slice."

So far, Susan had told me that Pamela had agreed to take her place at the gallery tomorrow, but she hadn't said a word about Chip.

"If you need anything, just ask Pamela," she said. "I'm afraid I haven't been much of a mentor. You've been left on your own."

"It hasn't been a problem. Ralph was there yesterday, but it wasn't really very busy." And I'd been so distracted over Susan's arrest that I'd let Ralph handle the few customers we'd had, but I didn't tell her that.

"I thought about coming in tomorrow, but I decided against it. I'm not quite ready to face the world yet. Everybody will be asking about my arrest. It's so embarrassing."

"The police are the ones who should be embarrassed," I declared.

"Exactly my thoughts. I can't begin to imagine who killed Janice, but here they are wasting time by focusing on me. I've racked my brain trying to think who might have wanted to kill her, but I can't come up with a clue."

"You did mention that lots of members have had disagreements with her."

"Yes, but that's par for the course anytime you get a group of artists together to run a co-op gallery. There's bound to be some friction. I can't see it escalating to the level of homicide, though."

"Maybe her death has nothing to do with the gallery at all," I suggested.

"I guess that's possible. It always seemed as though the gallery was her whole life, that she really didn't have a private life, but maybe that wasn't the case. She certainly never talked about her sister and, as far as I know, she never took a vacation."

Susan helped herself to another slice of cake. "I'm going to pig out here," she said. "This cake tastes so good. I love home-cooked food, but I don't often take the time to make any. It's so easy to stop in at Miguel's or call my brother and have Chip bring me a pizza or a calzone from the pizzeria. Speaking of Chip, I do want to talk to you about him."

"All right."

"Don't get me wrong. I love my nephew. The thing is, well, I'm afraid Chip's something of a ladies' man, or, at least, he'd like to be."

"Yes. I got that impression."

"Oh, so you know. That's good because I'd hate for you to get hurt. He's been talking about you quite a bit ever since he met you, which is a sure sign he's interested."

"He may be, but I'm certainly not! He's young enough to be my son. Believe me, I haven't encouraged him. He's shown up at my house unannounced a couple of times, but my son was there the first time and my neighbors, the second, so I couldn't really tell him I wasn't interested then."

"Oh, well, the best way is probably the direct approach. I can tell him, too, if you think that would help. He doesn't like to take 'no' for an answer, but if you're very firm, he will."

"Sounds as though you've been through this before."

"A few times, yes. Chip seems to be attracted to women who are older than he is, sometimes quite a bit older."

"I guess I fit that category."

"I wasn't thinking of you, Amanda. He dated my sixty-five-year-old neighbor for a while, then dropped her like a rock when he found someone else. She was really hurt. To this day, she avoids speaking to me. I guess I'm a reminder of him. He comes over here quite a bit, and whenever she sees him coming, she closes her blinds. Poor woman."

Chapter 20

Poor woman, indeed, I thought, as I drove home from Susan's. Maybe Chip wasn't so harmless, after all. If he didn't change his ways, he was bound to end up in hot water. I thought about warning Pamela, but my interference could easily backfire. She might assume I had a stake in the game and that I felt jealous.

I decided it was better to talk to Chip. I doubted very much that there was anything I could say that would convince him to mend his ways. Susan had already tried and failed. Persuading Chip that I wasn't interested in a romantic relationship with him was probably the most I could hope for.

Ironically, when I reported to the gallery for my morning shift the next day, Pamela and Chip were the first people I saw. I'd been expecting to see Pamela, but not Chip, so I wasn't unhappy when he left. As usual, he winked at me on his way out.

"Hi, Amanda. It looks as though it's just you and me this morning," Pamela said. "Judith is holed up in the office getting ready for her talk."

The blank expression on my face must have told Pamela I didn't know what she meant.

"About once a month or so, we invite an art class from the

high school to visit the gallery. Valerie, who's one of our board members, teaches art at LVHS. After the students look at the artwork in the gallery, they gather in our meeting room.

"Janice always used to talk to them about art as a career or a hobby. Judith said she'd do the same. It usually goes over pretty well. Of course, most of the students won't become professional artists, but I think it enhances their appreciation of art."

"Sounds like a good program."

Pamela nodded. "The class is due to arrive soon. We don't need to do anything special, just answer students' questions while they're looking around and keep an eye out for customers. When people see a crowd in the gallery, they often stop in."

"I guess I'll do some dusting before they arrive."

"So will I. Why don't you take the front, and I'll take the back," Pamela suggested.

It took only a few minutes for us to complete the chore.

"I noticed the police returned Janice's bear," Pamela said. "That's odd."

"No, they didn't return it. The one on display is a different bear. Judith put it out Friday."

"Ah, of course. It's one of Janice's limited editions."

"How did you know the police took it?" I asked. I remembered that Susan and I had been cautioned not to mention any details of what we'd observed at the crime scene even before Lieutenant Belmont had arrived to take charge.

"Someone must have told me, I guess. I can't remember who it was," she said, turning red. "Here comes the school bus now."

Pamela opened the gallery door and greeted Valerie and her students as they came in. Soon, the students were milling about the gallery.

Several of them snapped pictures of various artwork. Many

galleries didn't allow people to take photos of art on display; others, including the Roadrunner, did.

Maintaining a watchful eye on her students, Valerie told me that the students were required to write reports about a particular artwork of their choice or a review of an individual artist's body of work on display in the gallery. Valerie encouraged them to include images, as well as detailed descriptions, of the artwork in their reports.

As Pamela had predicted, the influx of students attracted the attention of passersby on Main Street, several of whom came into the gallery to browse. I noticed one woman lingering by Pamela's display. I thought Pamela could probably do a better job of pitching her painting than I could, but she hadn't noticed her potential customer because she was talking with a couple of students and had her back turned to the wall where her paintings hung.

I joined the three and let Pamela know she might have a buyer. She excused herself while I apologized to the students for the interruption.

"No problem. I get it," said one of the girls, who wore a distinctive strand of incised, blue ceramic beads. "My mom and I sell some of the jewelry we make at craft fairs. If someone looks interested, we always give them a sales pitch," she said knowingly. "I can usually tell by their body language if they're going to buy something."

"Hmm. I wish I had that talent. What do you think? Is that woman going to buy Pamela's painting?" I asked the student.

"Yeah, I think so."

Less than a minute later, Pamela removed her colorful painting of a tiger in the jungle and carried it to the counter next to the cash register.

"Told you," the girl said, as Pamela rang up the sale.

The unmistakable staccato click of high heels on the wooden floor interrupted us. Since most of the students wore thong sandals or sneakers, and I hadn't noticed anyone else wearing stilettos, I looked around to see where the noise was coming from.

It was Judith, back in the same designer shoes she'd discarded for her sister's more comfortable ones the last time I'd worked in the gallery. I supposed Judith thought the heels would look more professional for her speech to the art class, but as she tottered off with Valerie, leading the students to the gallery's meeting room, I wondered whether it wasn't more likely that she'd turn her ankle. After Belle's accident, I knew how serious that type of injury could be.

With the gallery now empty of students, it had suddenly become very quiet again. Pamela's customer left with her new painting, leaving Pamela and me alone in the gallery.

"Umm, Amanda. I, uh," Pamela began.

"What's up, Pamela?" I asked.

"This is awkward, but I hope I can count on your discretion."

I had a feeling I knew what was coming next.

"You may have seen something yesterday—something you weren't meant to see. You do know what I'm talking about, don't you?"

"Yes," I admitted.

"You didn't say a word when you came to my studio yesterday."

"It's your business, not mine. I was there to check the proof for the Friday night studio tour, not to spy on you. I just happened to come along at the wrong time, and I didn't want to embarrass us all by interrupting you."

"I understand. Of course, we didn't know you were there, but right after the students arrived, Chip called me to tell me he saw your car in the driveway yesterday. He didn't put two and two together until this morning when he spotted the same car outside the gallery after he left. I hope you haven't mentioned the incident to anybody."

"No."

"Well, thank you for that. I'd appreciate it if you would keep it to yourself."

"I plan to, Pamela, but I hope you know what you're doing. People could get hurt."

"You mean my husband?"

"I mean you *and* your husband."

"That's our problem," she snapped.

"I totally agree."

Pamela didn't respond. Perhaps she regretted bringing up the subject. I wished I'd never seen that kiss. The whole Pamela-Chip situation hit too close to home for me to look at it objectively. I didn't know Pamela's husband, but I realized I was identifying with his plight. I kept reminding myself that I knew Pamela only slightly and her husband not at all. I had no idea what their marriage was like. Best to mind my own business, I kept telling myself.

"Uh, oh, here comes trouble," Pamela said, nodding toward the gallery's entrance where a tall, distinguished-looking man, dressed in a bespoke suit, appeared. I did a double take, surprised to see Brooks Miller enter the Roadrunner.

I took a step forward to greet him, as we always did when people came into the gallery, but Pamela put her hand on my arm and shook her head, so I stopped.

Brooks ignored us as he methodically viewed each piece of artwork in the gallery, taking notes with a showy Waterman pen. Pamela and I retreated behind the counter while he made his rounds. When he finished, he approached us, ripped several pages from the small notebook he carried, and handed them to Pamela.

"See that the artists get these." It wasn't a request. It was a command.

"Don't I know you?" he asked me.

"We met last week when my son and I were having lunch at Cabo."

"Right, and you said you were local. You should think twice about being a member of this gallery. Associating with inferior artists never helps a painter's career."

I was literally speechless, but he didn't wait for my reply, anyway.

"What was that all about?" I asked Pamela.

"Brooks doing his quarterly critique."

"You mean those notes he gave you?"

"Yes. There's one for each painter. He doesn't bother with any of the other artists."

"He has a nerve."

"You must have seen his paintings."

"I have. When my son Dustin was visiting me last week, we went into his gallery. I don't know how he keeps the lights on. Does he actually sell that awful stuff?"

"He claims he does. Who knows? If you have enough money to subsidize your own business, I suppose it doesn't matter."

"I didn't realize he's wealthy. Isn't he the manager of the Lonesome Valley Resort, not the owner?"

"He's the manager, and his family trust owns the resort. I

wouldn't doubt that the Miller clan is the richest in Arizona."

"What do you do with his notes?"

"This," said Pamela, ripping the pages he'd scribbled in half and depositing them in the trash can. "From experience, I can tell you that he has absolutely nothing good to say. Constructive criticism is one thing; abuse is another. I don't know why we continue to put up with his asinine behavior. I've suggested to the board more than once that we should ban him from the gallery, but the other board members think taking action might lead to even more problems, so we do our best to ignore him."

"Ignore who?" Judith asked, as she joined us. I was surprised to see her because the high school art class hadn't yet left. I guessed they were still in the meeting room with Valerie.

"Brooks Miller. He owns the Brooks Miller Gallery on First Street," Pamela answered.

"Well, Mr. Miller gets around. His real estate agent visited me yesterday with an offer to buy this building, actually to trade it for the building that houses Miller's gallery plus a large sum of cash. It's an exceptionally good offer."

"I hope you're not considering it seriously," Pamela said, aghast. "We have the best location on Main Street."

"Yes. This is quite a good location, but may I remind you that the Roadrunner is here only because of my late sister's generosity. Yet, except for Travis, I haven't heard any of the members expressing regret at her loss."

"I assure you we all feel it deeply," Pamela said. "Perhaps the members don't want to upset you by talking about Janice."

"What about you, Amanda? Is that what you think?"

I felt like a deer in the headlights, being put on the spot like that.

Judith looked at me and said, "Oh, never mind. You haven't been here long enough to know which way is up." She stalked off, calling over her shoulder, "Let me know when the class is ready to leave."

Pamela and I didn't have a chance to speculate about Judith's comments because two couples came into the gallery just then. They wanted a recommendation for a good place to have lunch more than they wanted to look at art, but one of the women bought several note cards before they departed for the cafe Pamela had recommended.

I heard voices as Valerie came out of the meeting room and asked me to let Judith know that the class was ready to leave. I tapped on the office door and gave her the message. Judith gathered some cards from the credenza behind Janice's desk and handed one to each of the students as they filed out of the meeting room.

"Good for free art classes," one of them read from the card Judith had handed him. "Don't think so," he mumbled to himself as he stuffed the card into his jeans' pocket.

Other students reacted differently, though. I overheard several who sounded excited by the prospect of taking art classes at the Roadrunner.

"Did you ask Judith to donate the classes?" Pamela whispered to Valerie, as she was leaving.

"No. It was her own idea," Valerie replied. "I'm sure several of them will want to take advantage of the free offer. I don't have enough time to give them all a lot of one-on-one instruction, and some of them are very talented."

We watched as the class swarmed aboard the school bus.

"I think that went well," Judith said, waving to Valerie. "I'm going next door for coffee. Give me your orders, and I'll bring some back for you." I was glad that Judith's mood had lightened considerably. She seemed to have forgotten our earlier awkward conversation.

"What do you make of that?" I asked Pamela, after Judith left on her coffee run.

"Grief, I guess. That would account for her mood swings. I'm worried that she may actually be considering Miller's offer, though. There's really no reason for her to subsidize the gallery, like Janice did. Judith is used to running a for-profit, commercial gallery, and the co-op's a non-profit. It's an entirely different animal. If she sells, it could mean the end of the Roadrunner."

Chapter 21

My heart sank. Just as I was beginning to get established at the gallery, it might go under. I knew that the possibility was very real. Judith had called the offer "exceptionally good." She was a businesswoman who'd sold her Texas gallery for a pretty penny, so she should know. I wondered whether she was truly tempted by the prospect of a quick, lucrative sale. Maybe she was considering the offer because she thought the Roadrunner's members were ungrateful for all her sister had done for the gallery. After all the years of Janice's donating the gallery space to the co-op, perhaps they took it for granted, maybe even felt entitled to occupy the first floor of Janice's building.

Although those were both possibilities, I suspected that it had more to do with Judith's realization that the members wouldn't miss Janice much, despite Pamela's assertion that they felt her loss keenly. Even though the sisters had had a long estrangement, that knowledge must rankle. I doubted that Judith would have mentioned it if it hadn't.

"I don't know what we're going to do if she sells this building," Pamela said. "It wouldn't make any sense to move to the First Street location when many of the tourists never leave Main Street. As far as I know, there's no Main Street space available for lease or sale right at the moment. One solution would be for the co-op to buy this building, but, of course, we can't afford it. Each member would have to contribute thousands of dollars to make that happen. It's just not practical."

"I don't think it is, either. I know I couldn't afford to pay any more than I'm paying for the wall rental."

"I suppose my husband and I could buy the building, but I know I wouldn't be able to donate the gallery space. I'm sure my husband would agree only if it's a genuine investment. We'd have no problem finding a tenant for the apartment upstairs, but the co-op would also have to lease the gallery space. Even though that model could possibly work, we'd lose quite a few members because we'd have to raise the wall rental fee and take a commission on every sale. Perhaps we could attract some new members, though."

I could picture my future profits from sales in the gallery decreasing substantially if Pamela bought the place, but the alternative of moving the Roadrunner into the Brooks Miller Gallery would be even worse. Without the Main Street traffic, sales would undoubtedly dip considerably.

"How serious are you?" I asked Pamela.

"Dead serious. Can you imagine Brooks Miller's art in here? That's the only reason he wants to buy the building. He wants to take over the Roadrunner's space for his own gallery. I shudder at the prospect. When Judith comes back, I'm going to try to find out if she really intends to sell. If so, I'm going to ask her to allow me to top Miller's offer."

"What if she asks him to top *your* offer? From what you've told me, he has very deep pockets."

"If we end up in a bidding war, Miller will win; that's for

sure. It's just that I don't know what else to do. The Roadrunner's such a big part of my life, and now we might lose it."

Pamela looked as though she could burst into tears at any moment. Her bravado had dissolved in an instant.

"You know it's entirely possible that Judith is planning on keeping the building. She didn't come right out and say that she planned to sell it."

"You're right," Pamela said. "Maybe I'm getting ahead of myself, but why would she mention it if she isn't serious about selling?"

"I think maybe she wanted to tweak us a little. She's obviously unhappy that the members don't seem too upset about losing Janice."

"But everybody was shocked when they heard she was murdered right here in the gallery."

"Yes. That's true, but I wonder if she had any friends here because none of the members are talking about how much they'll miss her or what a great person she was, and I think Judith's picked up on their attitudes."

Pamela groaned. "You could be right. Janice knew a lot of people in the gallery and in the art world, but she probably didn't have any real friends. I can't say that I thought of her as a friend myself, and I've known her for years. She was such a strong-willed, controlling woman that it could be exhausting just interacting with her at the board meetings."

"So you never went out to lunch with her or invited her to join you for a social occasion?"

"I'm afraid not," she admitted, "and I can't think of anybody else who did. It's a sad commentary on her life, isn't it?"

"Yes, it is," I agreed.

"You're seeing the situation more clearly than I was. I never really thought about it before. Janice was, well, Janice, someone we had to accommodate so that she'd continue to donate the space for the Roadrunner. I guess we were using her in a way."

"Don't be so hard on yourself, Pamela. She was using the members, too. She got something out of it, probably the opportunity to play queen bee."

"Oh, brother. Too true. Here comes Judith with the coffee. Do you think I should ask her about the sale?"

"Maybe play it by ear. I have a feeling she might bring it up again to some of the other members, just to test the waters and see what kind of reaction she can provoke."

"I guess I'll hold off for now. I should talk to my husband about it, anyway."

That probably wasn't the only thing Pamela should talk to her husband about, I thought, but I didn't say anything. Judith was headed towards us, carrying a cardboard container with our drinks, and, besides, I had a mental vision of a huge neon sign flashing at me: MIND YOUR OWN BUSINESS!

"Here we are, ladies," Judith said, setting the container on the counter. "One mocha with whipped cream and one salted caramel macchiato." She handed me a long-handled plastic spoon. "For the mocha."

We thanked Judith and offered to pay for our drinks, but she wouldn't hear of it. She didn't tarry, but returned to her office, leaving us to speculate about her mercurial moods.

"Amanda, I want to apologize for speaking to you so sharply earlier. It isn't your fault you saw Chip and me kissing. After all, I asked you to come over to look at the proof for the Friday night studio tour. I really like Chip. He's a lot of fun, but I'm not sure how seriously he takes our relationship. I've heard some disturbing rumors. Supposedly, he asked Janice out several times. I just can't believe that, can you?"

I definitely could believe it, but I was spared from answering Pamela's question when Judith called Pamela to the phone in the office.

"It's a Mrs. Bramble," Judith said. "She says it's an emergency."

"My housekeeper," Pamela said, hurrying to the office.

"I have to leave," Pamela told us when she emerged. "A pipe burst, and Mrs. Bramble didn't notice it until our downstairs bathroom and family room were flooded. Will you be all right here by yourself, Amanda?"

"She won't be alone. I'll be here," Judith reminded Pamela, as we wished her good luck.

It was around noon when Pamela left, and although Judith and I greeted several visitors during the next hour, nobody bought anything. I recognized a couple of the women who came in because I'd seen them working in one of the boutiques down the block. I guessed that some of the other lookers were people who worked downtown and spent part of their lunch hour browsing.

Shortly before one o'clock, a couple of women I'd never seen before arrived for the afternoon shift. Dawn Martinez, the younger woman, appeared to be around my age and bore a resemblance to Dorothy Weber, the older lady, who I guessed was probably in her mid-seventies. I surmised they were mother and daughter, and when we introduced ourselves, they confirmed my suspicion. They told me they'd just returned from visiting relatives in California, which explained the reason we hadn't met before. Dorothy Weber and her daughter Dawn

Martinez both worked in clay, and their distinctive ceramic pieces went far beyond the run-of-the-mill bowls, platters, and vases that many potters made. Their pieces featured intricate applied decorations, glazed with their own special techniques. We chatted for a few minutes, and they invited me to tour their studio Friday night. I asked for a rain check since my own studio was now part of the Friday night tour lineup.

After Dorothy and Dawn signed in, I signed out. I lifted my purse from the deep drawer beneath the counter where we stowed our personal belongings while we were working, bade the mother-and-daughter duo good-bye, and headed for the door. Originally, I'd planned to go straight home after my shift at the gallery, but I didn't really need to. Laddie was enjoying Mr. Big's company, and Belle had encouraged me to take my time when I'd dropped Laddie off at her house that morning. Remembering Pamela's recommendation to the tourists who'd asked about a good place to eat, I decided to stop by the Valley Bread Bowl and treat myself to lunch there.

The payment from the judge and his wife had fattened my checking account, so I figured I didn't need to pinch pennies this week, although next week might be a different story. I might not have any more income for the rest of the month, and my rent would come due on the first. I'd already sold one of my paintings at the Roadrunner and I'd be paid for all my artwork that sold during April, but not until the tenth of May. Whether I'd sell any paintings during the Friday night studio tours remained to be seen, but I knew I couldn't count on it.

A year ago, I wouldn't have given a second thought to having a lunch out. Ned had taken care of our finances, and we'd never wanted for anything. I couldn't remember a time when he'd said we couldn't afford something, yet when it came time for our divorce settlement, there hadn't been any money. He must not have been as good a money manager as I'd thought. I supposed we must have spent the profits from the insurance agency as fast as we made them, and he'd borrowed what we needed to maintain our lifestyle. Money management had never really interested me, and I'd been happy enough to leave it to Ned, but now I regretted that decision because I wasn't very well prepared to deal with my own finances, and I feared I wasn't very good at it, either.

Judith was re-arranging a window display as I pushed the door open to leave.

"Think about framing your paintings, Amanda," she said. "It'll boost your sales."

I looked at her in surprise.

"Just a suggestion," she hastened to add. "Take it or leave it."

Smiling at her, I waved good-bye. I didn't want to be drawn into a discussion about framing or my finances, as had happened with her sister.

Outside the gallery, I put on my sunglasses. It was a gorgeous, warm, sunny day. Main Street looked festive with giant pots of flowers decorating the sidewalks, freshly painted benches where weary shoppers could rest, and hanging planters festooning the street lamps. I decided to walk the few blocks to the Valley Bread Bowl, even though I'd have to walk back later to retrieve my car.

I enjoyed window shopping as I passed by the stores on Main Street. Several of them had changed their displays since Dustin and I had browsed downtown just last week. I missed him, but I knew he had his own life to lead, and I wasn't as big a part of it as I had been when he was a child.

I missed Emma, too. It had been tough to adjust to her absence when she'd left for college her freshman year and even tougher last fall when she started her sophomore year, but since she planned to spend the summer with me, I could at least look forward to a long visit.

The wonderful aroma of baking bread wafted my way before I reached the restaurant. I thought it unusual because most eateries limit their baking to early morning hours, but the Valley Bread Bowl obviously didn't do that. No doubt the delicious smell of fresh-baked bread helped draw tourists and locals alike to the place.

When I entered, a large sign propped up on a tall easel invited me to seat myself. I went past a glass counter where loaves of bread were displayed and found a small booth away from the bright Arizona sunlight streaming through the plate glass windows in the front. I sat down facing the windows, but instantly realized my mistake and moved to the opposite side of the booth. The minute I removed my sunglasses, a server appeared. Her hair was pulled back in a neat bun, and she wore a spotless white apron and a pleasant smile as she handed me a menu and took my drink order for a large iced tea.

I scanned the menu that featured soup served in bread bowls and salads and sandwiches made from the restaurant's specialty breads. Although the hearty potato cheddar soup sounded good, it would have appealed to me more on a blustery winter day. I ordered an avocado and cheese sandwich, opting for plain whole wheat bread. The specialty breads appealed to me too, so I decided to buy a couple loaves to take home, one for me and another for Belle. As I ate my sandwich, I looked over the list of the restaurant's available breads.

"Mind if I join you?"

Since my back was turned to the restaurant's entrance, I hadn't seen Chip come in. Without waiting for my response, he slid into the booth, across from me. Luckily, I'd selected a small booth with room for only one person on each side. Otherwise, he might have decided to sit next to me.

My server materialized as soon as Chip sat down, and he ordered a large Pepsi.

"Amanda, I want to apologize for not meeting you at the courthouse yesterday. Everything was happening so fast. We wanted to take Aunt Susan home right away when we found out she was going to be released from jail, and I forgot to let you know. She told me you brought her dinner last night. That was thoughtful. You're a nice lady."

He flashed his boyish grin at me, but I didn't smile back because I didn't want to encourage him. So far, he'd done all the talking, but it was time for me to speak up and set him straight.

"Chip, don't try to butter me up."

He opened his mouth to protest, but I continued before he had a chance to interrupt me. "We're colleagues at the Roadrunner, but that's all. I'm not interested in going out with you, and I don't want you to show up at my house out of the blue again."

"But I thought . . . why did you agree to meet me at the courthouse?"

"To give Susan moral support, like you said."

"Uh, huh." His tone indicated he didn't believe me, or maybe he just didn't want to believe me. "If our age difference bothers you, don't let it. I prefer older women. They're so much more interesting than girls my age."

I shook my head in disbelief. He didn't seem to be getting the message.

"OK, I get it. If that's not what's bothering you, I think I know what the problem is. You saw me with Pamela yesterday; I can explain."

"There's no need to explain," I said.

"I want to. Pamela's a wonderful woman, but she's gotten kind of clingy lately. I'll let her down gently if you'll agree to go out with me."

Chapter 22

"Chip, no!" I said in exasperation. "Don't you dare use me as an excuse to break up with Pamela or for any other reason. Once and for all, I'm not attracted to you, and I don't want to date you. Case closed."

Chip pulled a mock pouty face. "Your dog likes me."

"My dog would lead a burglar to my diamond jewelry collection, if I had one. He's very friendly."

"More than I can say for you,"

I couldn't help noticing that Chip didn't exactly seem devastated.

"Chip, I hope you realize your flirting could lead to big trouble."

"That's what Aunt Susan says. I don't see the harm in having fun myself."

"Having fun's one thing; hurting people is another."

"Oh, so you're looking for a *serious* relationship? OK, scout's honor, I can do that."

Even though I could tell that he was teasing now, I couldn't let his declaration go. "No! Honestly, Chip, you're incorrigible. I know you're not serious, so knock it off."

"Oh, but I can be very serious."

"I doubt that," I replied, signaling to the server for my check. When she delivered it, along with the two loaves of bread I'd ordered, I noticed that Chip's Pepsi was included on the bill. It was only a minor annoyance, but Mr. Charm hadn't offered to pay for it, and I had no intention of asking him for the few dollars it cost.

After I slid my credit card into the folder with the bill, I turned it sideways and put it on the edge of the table so that she'd notice it was ready. She soon spotted it and whisked it away.

While we waited for her to come back so that I could sign my receipt, I decided to change the subject. "By the way, Chip, does anyone ever call you Travis? You were introduced to me as Travis at my membership interview, and I noticed that you sign your paintings Travis Baxter."

"Just my mom when she's mad at me and Janice. She always used to call me Travis. I guess she thought Chip didn't sound dignified enough for an artist of my elevated status." He dropped his jokester persona for a minute. "She was like a mentor to me. I'll miss her."

"You may be the only one from what her sister said this morning. Judith was complaining that the Roadrunner members don't feel sorry to have lost Janice. Pamela tried to tell her otherwise, but I don't know whether she believed her. Judith's had an offer to purchase the building. It almost seemed like a threat when she talked about the possibility of selling it."

"I don't like the sound of that," Chip said. "Janice never would agree to selling the building. She had several offers from Brooks Miller, but I know she didn't ever consider selling because the Roadrunner was her life. Do you know if this offer came from Brooks?"

"Yes, she said it did."

"That guy just won't quit. I wonder if Judith's seen his so-called artwork. If she has, I don't understand how she could possibly think about selling the building. It's bad enough that he has a gallery on First Street. It would be a travesty to move it to Main Street."

Even though I couldn't help smiling at his feeble pun, I had to agree. Having the Brooks Miller Gallery in a prime location on Main Street wouldn't enhance the reputation of Lonesome Valley's downtown district.

Suddenly Chip jumped up. "Gotta go. Dad will be on my case if I'm late for work again. See you later, Amanda, and thanks for the Pepsi."

He'd expected me to pay for it, I realized, just as he assumed any older woman he liked would cater to him. I suspected that's exactly what his mother did, but his little-boy charm tactics evidently didn't work on his father.

Before I left the restaurant, I texted Belle to let her know I'd be home soon. On my way out, I stopped at the bread case in front and picked out a couple of appealing loaves. As I walked back to my car, I didn't linger to look in the shop windows. Back at home, I checked on Mona Lisa, but she refused to come down from her kitty perch even though I put a snack in her bowl. I knew she'd eat it the minute I left, so I went next door, taking both loaves of bread with me.

Laddie and Mr Big ran to greet me at Belle's front door.

"They just woke up from a long nap," Belle told me. "What do you have there?"

"Bread from the Valley Bread Bowl. Which one would you like? I have sweet, the cinnamon raisin bread, or savory, the olive-cheddar bread."

"I'll go with the olive-cheddar loaf. Thanks, Amanda. You'll have to try some later. It's really good. I haven't been to the Bowl lately, but I do love their bread."

Laddie and Mr. Big followed Belle to the kitchen as she took the olive-cheddar loaf and put it in the pantry. They knew she kept a stash of dog biscuits in there, too. Belle didn't disappoint them, handing each dog a bone-shaped biscuit, a tiny one for Mr. Big and a large one for Laddie.

"I was thinking maybe we could take the dogs to the park, but only if you feel like it," Belle suggested. "You've probably been on your feet all morning."

"Actually we probably sat behind the counter about half the time I was there, and I could use some exercise." My six-block walk downtown hadn't really been very strenuous, and I didn't feel the least bit tired. "But are you sure you're up to it? What about your ankle?"

"I'm doing better. Dennis and I took Mr. Big for a short walk last night, and it didn't bother me."

"OK. Well, if it starts to hurt, I can always come back to get the car and pick you up."

"Right. I think I can make it to the park and back. Knock on wood." Belle tapped her knuckles on her oak dining table.

Laddie and Mr. Big wriggled with anticipation as we clipped their leashes to their collars and set out for the park. I hoped Belle wasn't being too ambitious, but I noticed her limp wasn't as pronounced as it had been a few days before.

"Belle, I want to ask your opinion about something," A crazy idea had occurred to me, and I couldn't stop thinking about it, but maybe when I said it out loud, I could make some sense of it. I wanted to hear Belle's reaction.

"Sure, what is it, Amanda?"

"This is going to sound totally weird, but hear me out."

"OK," she said slowly, drawing the word out.

"I don't think Janice was murdered."

"You mean you think her death was an accident?"

"No, I mean maybe it wasn't Janice who died. Remember I told you Janice's twin sister has taken over as gallery director?"

"Right."

"I think maybe Judith was the one who was killed, and Janice is pretending to be her own twin."

Belle looked at me in astonishment.

"I know it sounds far-fetched, but I've noticed some things. Maybe they don't mean anything, but let me tell you and see what you think."

"I'm all ears."

"First of all, there's the matter of her shoes. Janice always wore comfortable shoes with crepe soles. I never saw her wear anything else. When Judith made her first appearance here at our members' meeting at the library last week, she wore high heels, and I remember that she stumbled on her way to the podium. Then, at the gallery the other day, she wore stilettos at first, but later she changed into Janice's shoes. She claimed she was concerned about her heels marring the wooden floor in the gallery, but we have customers who wear all sorts of footwear, so that didn't seem completely plausible to me.

"This morning, she started out wearing Janice's shoes again, but when she went to the meeting room to speak to a high school art class that was visiting the gallery, she wore high heels, and she was struggling in them. She did not look like a woman who was used to wearing them, but I guess she thought she should try because that's what Judith always wore."

"I grant you, that's a little odd, but how do you know what Judith wore?"

"After the meeting at the library, I looked her up online, out of curiosity. There are dozens of pictures of her on the web, and she's wearing heels in every one of them."

"Hmm. Could be she's nervous and wobbly, on edge because of her sister's murder."

"That's true, but there's more. This morning she made the comment that I'd been at the gallery for 'about a minute,' as she put it."

Belle looked confused.

"She meant I hadn't been a member very long. Now how did she know that?"

"She could have read the membership records."

"I suppose. It's not the first thing I'd do if my sister had been murdered right there in the gallery, but she could have checked them I guess."

"What else?"

"When I left the gallery today, Judith told me to think about framing my paintings, that I'd sell more if I did. That, in itself, wouldn't have been unusual, but Janice told me the same thing. In fact, she made a big issue of it the day I hung my paintings at the gallery."

"The two could think alike, you know. After all, they're identical twins, and both have been in the gallery business for years."

"Right. It's just that Judith seems more than a little familiar with the Roadrunner and its operations. When she noticed Janice's bear sculpture was missing from its pedestal, she replaced it immediately with another one from the same limited edition. If she hadn't known exactly where to find it, she couldn't have produced it so quickly"

I looked at Belle, and the doubt on her face was plain to see.

"You're not convinced yet, are you?"

"All those things seem a little strange, but they can all be explained."

"Oh, and Judith called Chip 'Travis.' Chip told me that Janice was the only person who always called him Travis, except for his mother when she's irritated with him—oh, and Pamela called him that, too, once at the library meeting, but I'm pretty sure that was only because she wanted to keep it formal."

"Amanda, you may be reading too much into these incidents."

"My over-active imagination's running wild, huh?"

"Not necessarily, but has anyone else noticed or mentioned anything strange about Judith's behavior?"

"Not a soul. But don't you see? If I'm right, she could still be in danger. If Janice is impersonating her twin, and the killer figures it out . . . ."

"I understand. That's assuming Janice was meant to be the target all along. There must be a way to find out Judith's identity. Maybe someone who's known Janice for a long time could offer some insight."

"That's just it. All the other gallery members have known her longer than I have, and they haven't been suspicious."

Chapter 23

We walked in silence for a few minutes, pondering the situation. By this time, we'd reached the park. Laddie and Mr. Big pulled at their leashes until we stepped off the sidewalk so that they could roll in the grass. After he jumped up, Mr. Big started yelping.

We looked around to see what he was barking at and spotted Rebecca with her two terriers. She saw us, too, and waved. We walked toward each other until we met near the park shelter. We played out the dogs' leashes, and they tumbled around each other until their leads were all in a tangle, and we had to straighten them out.

After their encounter, Laddie and the terriers cooperated nicely by lying in the grass, but Mr. Big had other ideas. He wanted to play, and he refused to settle down until Belle picked him up. Cradling him in her arms, she sat down at one of the picnic tables. He wiggled for a while, but Belle held him tightly, and he soon gave up his struggle, although he continued to maintain a watchful eye on us while Belle kept him calm by petting him.

"He's a pistol," Belle commented.

"He certainly is an energetic little guy," Rebecca agreed. "How's your ankle?"

"Much better, thanks. It feels good to rest it, though."

While we chatted with Rebecca, I tried to think of a subtle way to ask her about Judith. Finally, I decided to come right out with it. She might think I was crazy, but she'd known the twins in high school, perhaps longer than any members of the Roadrunner had known Janice, and she might be able to help.

"Rebecca, have you heard from Judith since she came back to town?"

"No. I called the gallery the other day, just to find out if anyone had heard from her, and they told me she's taken Janice's place as gallery director. I left a message for her, but she never returned my call, so yesterday I went to the gallery, hoping to catch her, but she wasn't in. Or so I was told. I got the feeling the woman who told me that was covering for Judith. She probably said she didn't want to see anyone. I'm sure Janice's death hit her hard. So far as I know, the two never reconciled."

"Would you be willing to try again?"

"I plan on it. Why do you ask?"

"Well . . . ." I took a deep breath and explained. To my surprise, Rebecca began nodding her head as she listened to my speculations.

"It's possible, Amanda," Rebecca told me. "When we were in high school, Janice and Judith switched places and pretended to be each other several times. Even their own father couldn't always tell them apart, but their mother was never fooled."

"How about you?"

"I wasn't fooled either. Back then, I could always tell them apart. I can't exactly pinpoint how I knew. Intuition, I suppose."

"Wow!" Belle exclaimed, "and here I've been playing devil's

advocate. It sounds as though you might be right, Amanda."

"We need to find out."

"Why don't I go down to the gallery right now? This time I'll peek in the window to make sure Judith's there before I go in. I'd better get going before Dennis comes back from the hardware store. I don't want him to find out about our suspicion. You know how concerned he is about the murder happening here in town. He might think it's dangerous for us to be poking around. I'll call you after I've seen Judith or Janice, as the case may be."

We round robined our phones, entering our contact information, so that the three of us could keep in touch. When Rebecca hurried off, Belle loosened her grip on Mr. Big, and he jumped off her lap to follow his terrier buddies, but she had his leash firmly in hand, and he didn't get far. We circled the park and then headed for home. I worried that the walk had been too much for Belle because she was limping more noticeably the last block before home.

Belle refreshed the water in the dogs' bowls, grabbed two bottles of water from the refrigerator, and handed one to me. We sat down in the living room, where Belle put her feet up on the sofa and propped a pillow under her ankle.

"Do you want an ibuprofen?" I asked Belle.

"No. I may have overdone it, just a bit, but I'll be fine," she said optimistically. "I just need to rest a while."

Our phones beeped simultaneously. Rebecca had texted us both that she'd seen Judith through the gallery's front window, and she was about to go inside.

We waited anxiously to hear back from her. It wasn't long before my phone rang. I quickly punched "speaker" so that Belle would be able to hear both sides of our conversation.

"It's a no-go, I'm afraid," Rebecca said. "I'm walking back to my car now."

"You mean Judith's not really Janice?"

"I didn't get close enough to tell. When I went into the gallery, Judith started to come towards me. I'm sure she recognized me, but she turned around, said something to the man who was there, and took off. She disappeared around a corner, and I heard a door close."

"Probably went to the office," I said.

"I think she went upstairs to the apartment. I could hear footsteps. Anyway, I told the man I was an old friend of Judith's and that I'd like to see her, but he said she wouldn't be in the gallery for the rest of the day."

"Now what do we do?" Belle asked.

"I could try again tomorrow," Rebecca offered, "but obviously she's deliberately avoiding me."

"Maybe that's because she doesn't want her impersonation revealed."

"My interest is really piqued now," Rebecca said. "I'm going to try to catch her off-guard tomorrow, if possible. Does she ever leave the gallery?"

"I suppose she must. This morning she went next door for coffee."

"I could stake out the coffee shop. Even though we've been out of touch for several years, I can't believe Judith wouldn't want to see me. She's one of my oldest friends. Let me think about the best way to contact her, and I'll keep you posted."

Rebecca hung up, leaving us as much in the dark as we'd been before, although Belle and I agreed that Judith's avoidance of Rebecca seemed suspicious.

"Tell Dennis I'm making the first installment on my

payment plan this evening," I told Belle before Laddie and I left. She looked confused for a moment before she smiled.

"Chocolate, apricot, or pecan?" she asked.

"Chocolate meringue tonight, since that was Dennis's first choice."

"Great! We'll look forward to it."

By the time we returned home, Mona Lisa had decided she'd missed us. Instead of observing us from her perch, she came running when we walked in the door. She greeted Laddie with a plaintive "meow" that conveyed her how-dare-you-leave-me attitude before she executed a series of figure eights around my ankles. It was too early for their dinner, but when my pets looked at me hopefully, I caved and gave Laddie a few carrots and Mona Lisa a kitty treat. They both settled themselves on the kitchen floor, making progress in the tiny room difficult, but I didn't have the heart to shoo them away while I assembled the ingredients for the pie. During Dustin's visit, I'd made some extra pasty shells and frozen them, so I took one of them out of the freezer to thaw while I made the filling and whipped up the meringue topping.

After I put the pie into the oven to brown the meringue, I went into the living room, Laddie and Mona Lisa at my heels, and turned on the television to catch the local news. According to the reporter for Channel 2, there had been no new developments in the investigation of Janice's murder. A brief clip of an interview with the police chief elicited the information that the investigation was ongoing. Lieutenant Belmont was nowhere in sight.

The timer on the stove buzzed, alerting me to check the pie. When I peeked into the oven, I was pleased that the meringue had turned a perfect golden brown. I carefully removed it from the oven and set it on a rack to cool.

Laddie and Mona Lisa hadn't forgotten their dinner, and they lurked in the kitchen until I filled their bowls and fed them. After the large sandwich I'd consumed for lunch, I wasn't terribly hungry myself, so I made an omelet and toasted a slice of the cinnamon bread I'd brought home from the Valley Bread Bowl for my own dinner. I was happy to have found the restaurant. Its bread was delicious, and it would be fun sampling the different varieties now that I'd discovered the place.

When my smartphone rang, I half-expected that Rebecca was calling again, but Susan's face appeared on the display instead. If she'd been arrested again, she wouldn't be calling me on her cell phone, so I took her call as a good sign.

"Hi, Amanda. I have some news."

Susan sounded better, more like herself.

"What's up?"

"A couple of things. First of all, my lawyer talked to the district attorney again and found out that the witness who reported seeing me going into the gallery early the day Janice was killed may not be a witness at all. The police got an anonymous phone call. They don't know who made it, and I guess they've canvassed all the people who work in shops near the gallery, and nobody saw a thing."

"That call could have been made by the killer to throw the police off."

"That's what my lawyer said. The only thing they have against me is my threat to kill Janice, but that happened two years ago. Of course, I didn't mean it literally, and I was stupid to say it in the first place. I remember how angry I was with Janice that day, but I never should have said that I could kill her. Our argument must have made quite an impression. I guess several of the gallery members reported the incident when Belmont questioned them."

"Not much to build a case on."

"No. My lawyer said not to worry. If all they can come up with is a two-year-old threat I made in the heat of the moment, the district attorney won't charge me."

"Thank goodness for that."

"To tell you the truth, I'm still embarrassed to go out in public. I'm the only person I know who's spent a night in jail. I feel like a criminal, even though I haven't committed any crime, but I can't hide in the house forever, which brings me to the other reason I called you."

"Umm, hmm?"

"The Roadrunner has a booth in the Lonesome Valley Spring Arts and Crafts Fair this weekend. It's not one of our bigger events, since it's more focused on crafts than art, but we always participate. It helps to publicize the gallery, and we sell a few items, mostly cards and prints, but once in a while a painting. Anyway, this event has been scheduled for months, and Tiffany and I volunteered to staff the booth for the weekend, but she's developed a bad case of bronchitis, so she won't be able to help. I was wondering if you'd consider filling in on Saturday."

"Sure. I can do that, but what about Sunday?"

"Pamela's agreed to help, too, but she can't be there Saturday, so with you helping out, we'll be fine. By the way, Chip and Lonnie will set up our tent, the tables, and our grids, so we won't have to lift anything heavy. You can hang a couple of smaller paintings and bring some note cards and prints, if you like."

"I'll do that. I know just the paintings to bring. They're both sixteen by twenty inches. Will that size work?"

"Perfectly. The weather forecast looks promising. It's always so miserable if the weather turns cold and rainy, and wind can be even worse, but I think we'll be fine."

After promising to get back to me with our booth's location, Susan rang off. She seemed to be looking forward to the fair, despite her reluctance to be seen in public. It certainly sounded as though she wasn't going to be charged, so I hoped that working at the fair would help her ease back into her routine.

She hadn't mentioned Chip except to tell me that he would help. I assumed he wouldn't hang around after he and Lonnie set up our tent, grids, and tables, but, if so, at least I wouldn't have to be alone with him. Susan would be there as a buffer. I had a feeling that Chip hadn't taken me seriously when I told him I didn't feel attracted to him.

Chapter 24

Although I'd planned to spend most of the day Thursday in my studio painting, I kept turning the idea of Janice's masquerading as Judith over and over in my mind. At times I convinced myself that Janice was impersonating her twin, but at other times, I thought about how her actions could have other logical explanations, as Belle had pointed out.

Given my propensity for procrastination, combined with my curiosity about our new gallery director, I had no problem agreeing when Rebecca called to suggest that I try to entice Judith to accompany me to the coffee shop where Rebecca would be waiting. I would have suggested that Belle come along, but I knew that her morning was already booked at her hairdresser's salon, followed by a doctor's appointment.

I needed to think of some plausible reason for me to show up at the gallery since I wasn't scheduled to work there again until the following week. If I replaced one of my paintings with a different landscape, none of the members would think twice about it, so I selected a moody, ethereal piece done in soft hues of gray punctuated by some bright areas of fuchsia, viridian green, and gold ochre. Since my landscapes tended to be brighter and more colorful than my newest addition, I hadn't hung it in the gallery initially, but maybe its atmospheric quality would appeal to a potential buyer.

"I didn't breath a word about our stakeout to Greg," Rebecca said when she picked me up. "I told him we were going to meet for coffee. I think he felt a little disappointed that I didn't ask him to come along, but as soon as I mentioned that we might also do some shopping, his interest waned immediately. If there's anything Greg hates, it's shopping." She chuckled. "By the way, that's a beautiful painting, Amanda. It would look fabulous in our guestroom. How much are you asking for it?"

When I named the price, Rebecca gasped, "Oh, really? I had no idea paintings were so expensive." She hastened to add, "not that they're not worth it. I've never bought one; that's all. How long did it take you to paint this one?"

"I spent about fifty hours on it."

"No wonder it's pricey. You'll have to forgive my ignorance, Amanda. I really had no idea. Obviously, I don't know much about art. When we were in high school, Judith and Janice took the art classes. I was in the choir. Still am, for that matter—church choir and the Lonesome Valley Pioneers. We give a couple of concerts every year, and sometimes we sing at local events. We're going to be at the arts and crafts fair Saturday."

"Me, too. The gallery will have an exhibit there. What time are you performing?"

"One o'clock, in the park pavilion."

"I'll try my best to get over there to see the choir if they can spare me for a while. I don't know whether our spot will be close to the pavilion or not."

"And I'll come over to the gallery's exhibit afterwards. Well, here we are," Rebecca said as she parked a few doors away from the coffee shop. "I hope I'll be able to snag a booth in there. It looks busy."

We entered the coffee shop and found a place to sit right away. "Why don't you wait here to save the booth while I order a coffee," Rebecca suggested.

When she returned with a large cup of coffee, we strategized. I would invite Judith to come with me to the coffee shop. Once she entered, she wouldn't be able to avoid Rebecca, and the two could talk while I ordered coffee and made myself scarce, giving Rebecca a chance to size up Judith.

We had no idea whether our simple plan would work, but we were ready to give it a try.

"Here goes nothing," I said to Rebecca as I picked up my painting.

When I entered the gallery, Ralph was sitting behind the counter, and Judith was nowhere to be seen.

"Good morning, Ralph," I said. "Is Judith around?"

"In the office."

"You're not here alone today, are you?"

"No. Carrie's in the meeting room, organizing the note cards and prints we'll be taking to the arts and crafts fair this weekend."

"Thanks, Ralph. I'm going to help out at the fair. Maybe I should check with her." I wandered back to the meeting room. I couldn't go into the room without thinking about my membership interview there, not a pleasant memory for me.

"Carrie, hi. I'm Amanda. I think we met a couple of weeks ago."

"Oh, right. You're our new landscape painter. What can I help you with?"

"I'll be at the fair with Susan for part of the weekend. Should

I take my note cards and prints to the fair Saturday, or do you need to organize them here?"

"You can take them Saturday. As long as everything is packaged with your name and the item's price, we can keep tabs on our sales."

"OK, thanks." I left Carrie arranging prints by size in boxes and went back into the gallery, where I swapped the painting I'd brought for another of the same size on my wall.

"Lovely painting, Amanda."

I jumped. With the crepe-soled shoes she wore, Judith hadn't made a sound when she'd come up behind me.

"I didn't mean to startle you," she continued without waiting for a response. "The gallery's quiet this morning, but I expect we'll have a good weekend."

Grabbing my opportunity, I agreed that it was quiet. It seemed like the perfect time to invite Judith for coffee.

"Would you like to join me for coffee, Judith? I'm just going next door to the Coffee Klatsch. We can bring something back for Ralph and Carrie."

"No, thanks, Amanda. I've already had my fill of coffee this morning, but I'm sure Ralph and Carrie would appreciate it."

Desperately, I tried to think of a way to change her mind, but I wasn't that quick on my feet. I drew a blank.

As Judith turned and began to walk away, I called, "Janice!"

Without hesitation, she turned, "Yes?" It took a few seconds for her to realize she'd answered to her own name, rather than Judith's. Then she tried to make light of her gaff, but I didn't buy it for a minute.

Janice stood there, looking at me. "Judith" had been Janice all along!

Chapter 25

We stared at each other, neither of us breaking eye contact until a commotion at the front of the gallery distracted us. When Janice went to investigate, I quickly pulled my cell phone out of my pocket and tapped it to call Rebecca.

"Rebecca, you'd better come over to the gallery right away," I told her. "Janice just gave herself away, although she won't admit it. If she sees you, maybe we'll get somewhere."

"I'll be right there."

I slipped my phone back into my pocket and went to the front. With one of us behind her and the other in front of her, Janice wouldn't be able to worm her way out of the situation too easily when Rebecca arrived. I could hear Janice's raised voice coming from the front of the gallery. As soon as I went around the wall that divided the gallery, I saw the source of the problem.

Brooks Miller had blustered his way in, and now he and Janice were engaged in a heated argument while Ralph watched them from behind the counter, his hand on the telephone.

"This is another one of your ploys to get me to raise my offer again," Brooks said angrily. "You're not going to get a better price. I'm offering twice what this building's worth, and you know it."

"Maybe I don't want to sell."

"You stupid woman," Brooks yelled in frustration. "You'll sell this building to me or you'll regret it."

"That sounds like a threat, Miller. Get out! Now!" Ralph said.

"I'm not going anywhere. Not till she comes to her senses and signs the contract my agent presented."

"Mr. Miller," Ralph said. "You heard the lady. You're not welcome here. Now you have two seconds to get to the front door before I call the police. I have 9-1-1 on speed dial." Ralph picked up the receiver and curled his gnarled index finger above the push button on the landline's old-fashioned phone. When Brooks didn't budge, Ralph jabbed the button.

Brooks, his face contorted with rage, strode toward the front entrance just as Rebecca opened the door to come in.

"I wouldn't sell this building to you if you were the last man on earth," Janice yelled.

Brooks pushed past Rebecca and left the gallery. We could hear the siren of a police car close by, but by the time Mike, the young patrol officer, arrived, Brooks had vanished. At some point, Carrie had joined us, although, in the excitement, I hadn't noticed her at first. Janice cast a wary eye at Rebecca as Ralph explained to Mike why he'd made the 9-1-1 call.

"I didn't know what he was going to do, Officer Dyson," Ralph said. "He threated Judith, so I asked him to leave. When he refused, I made the call."

I noticed that Janice let Ralph do the talking. She'd looked startled when she first saw Mike, even though she knew Ralph had called the police.

"Ms. Warren, do you have anything to add?" He asked the question while staring down at the small notebook he held in his hand. He never looked directly at Janice.

"No," she said quietly.

"Anybody else have something to add?"

Nobody responded.

"And you're sure it was Brooks Miller, the guy from the Lonesome Valley Resort?"

"And the Brooks Miller Gallery," I added. "It was him all right. No doubt about it."

"OK, got it. Thanks, Amanda." Mike flashed me a brief smile. "I'll report this incident right away, but it'll probably be the detective who investigates, given what happened here last week. That's about all I can tell you. I suppose he could be charged with trespass or disturbing the peace, but it'll be up to the district attorney."

"He won't be charged with a thing if I don't miss my guess," Ralph grumbled. "The district attorney likes to keep the powers that be happy."

"Well, I don't know about that," Mike responded. "But it's not my call."

"Understood, Officer. We appreciate the fast response."

After noting all our names and contact information, Mike left. The flashing lights of the police car sitting outside the gallery had attracted some attention, and a small crowd had gathered outside, but as soon as Mike left, the curiosity seekers went their separate ways. A few came into the gallery, probably more to find out what had happened than to look at the art. Ralph, Carrie, and Janice approached the visitors while I hung back with Rebecca so that we'd have a chance to confer.

"What do you think?" I asked. "Is she Janice?"

"No doubt about it," Rebecca answered.

"How sure are you?"

"One hundred percent. She's definitely Janice. I was afraid that maybe after all these years, I wouldn't be able to tell Janice and Judith apart, but I was wrong." Tears flooded Rebecca's eyes as she said, "Judith's gone. My friend is dead."

The woman who'd been talking to Janice left. When Janice looked at us, she saw Rebecca crying. I wondered whether she'd deny impersonating Judith to her twin's oldest friend.

"Let's go upstairs to my apartment, ladies," she said wearily. We followed her as she trudged up the stairs. Janice unlocked her apartment door, and we went inside, through a narrow entry way that opened onto her spacious living room.

The plush sofa, ottoman, and chairs looked comfortable, but it was the life-size bronze of a mountain lion perched on a ledge that jutted out from one wall that dominated the room. The big cat's languid pose belied its predatory expression. Although it was lying down with its tail draped over the ledge where it rested, its head was raised as it surveyed its domain.

The display had a museum-like quality because the entire wall behind the mountain lion was a mural of a realistic Arizona mountain habitat, yet the background painting didn't overwhelm its focal point, the bronze cougar. I moved closer to the wall to look at the details of the painter's work. I almost missed seeing the signature because I hadn't been looking at the bottom of the painting, but the artist had signed his work. His name stood out, rendered in bold confident strokes: Travis Baxter.

It was then that I realized I'd never seen any of Chip's artwork before. Although he was a member of the Roadrunner's board, none of his paintings hung in the gallery.

As though reading my mind, Janice offered an explanation.

"Travis is a talented artist, but he's having a difficult time finding the right direction for his art. I believe he should concentrate on murals, and I've tried to guide him, but his work ethic isn't what it should be if he wants to find success in this business. If he'd settle down and concentrate, he'd do much better, but he's too easily distracted."

"We're not here to talk about art," Rebecca snapped. "Why are you impersonating Judith? Did you kill your sister?"

"Of course not." Janice looked horrified. "I'm trying to find out who did. Whoever it was wanted *me* dead, not Judith."

"How do you know that?" Rebecca asked.

"Oh, come on, Rebecca. Who was always the popular twin? Everyone loved Judith. Amanda can tell you how much the members of the Roadrunner miss me—they don't. Besides, I doubt that anyone knew she was in Lonesome Valley. I certainly wasn't expecting her."

"But I don't understand how you hope to find her killer by pretending to be Judith. That doesn't make sense," I said. "Why not let the police handle the investigation? That's their job."

"And they're doing such a splendid one," Janice said sarcastically. "Look who they arrested. Susan's a wimp. She'd be too scared to hurt anyone, even if she wanted to."

"She once threatened to kill you," I reminded her.

"I didn't take that threat seriously. Anyway, it was two years ago. We haven't had any major disagreements in quite a while. No, it isn't Susan, but I have an idea who it might be."

"Then if you have evidence, take it to the police," I urged. "Let them sort it out."

"That's the thing. I have suspicions, not hard evidence."

"Go on."

"Well, take Brooks Miller, for example. He'd like nothing

better than to move his gallery into the Roadrunner. We have a prime Main Street location that can't be beat. He's been trying for years to convince me to sell, but I always refuse. Maybe he thought that, with me out of the way, he'd have an easier time negotiating a deal."

"But now, as Judith, you're still not agreeing to sell."

"I'm toying with him. I wanted to see how he'd react. I told his real estate agent that I was inclined to sell, and you saw how Brooks reacted a few minutes ago when I told him that maybe I didn't want to. He went ballistic. The man has a temper. If you ask me, he's capable of commiting murder. I'm going to see how far I can push him. If he comes after me, I'll know he's the murderer."

"Deliberately putting yourself in danger is a terrible plan, Janice," I protested.

"I'm armed, remember?"

"You're not honoring Judith's memory by playing your preposterous game when you should be planning Judith's funeral, instead," Rebecca told her.

"I fully intend to hold a memorial service for Judith, but not until I find her killer."

"You always were the stubborn one, Janice."

While Rebecca and Janice argued, I thought about what Janice had said earlier.

"Janice, would a man like Brooks Miller really go to such lengths as murder in hopes of buying this building? I don't know that your theory holds up. He obviously has plenty of money. It's not as though his livelihood's in jeopardy."

"Brooks has a huge ego, and he's dead set on moving into the Roadrunner's space. His money didn't help him get what he wanted, so he took another path."

"I suppose it's possible," I said dubiously, "but not very likely."

"Well, someone killed my sister," Janice snapped. "Brooks isn't the only person with a motive."

"Oh?"

"I think he's the most likely suspect, but there's someone else."

"Who?"

"You were at the members' meeting at the library, Amanda. Ask yourself this: who wanted to be gallery director?"

"Pamela. You think *she* murdered Judith?" I was flabbergasted. "You're saying Pamela killed Judith, thinking she was you, because she wants to be gallery director?"

"That's one motive. The other is her jealousy of me."

"Because you're the gallery director?"

"Because Travis loves me."

I thought Rebecca was going to fall out of her chair at that statement. Janice flashed a smug look at Rebecca.

"You thought a man could never be attracted to me, didn't you? High school was forty years ago, Rebecca. Time to get over it."

"Pamela said she'd heard rumors," I mused. "So you and Chip were having an affair while he was dating Pamela."

"No. That's not what I said. Travis loves me, but we're not lovers. I'm not foolish enough to get involved with him romantically, no matter how many times he suggests it. No, our relationship is much stronger than that. I mentor him; we can talk about anything. I consider him my protégé, but I doubt that Pamela could understand."

"She's such a petite woman. I can't picture her being strong enough to murder anybody," I said, "even if she was terribly jealous and meant to do harm."

Janice shrugged. "She probably didn't. All I'm saying is she's a suspect. I think it's far more likely that Brooks is the killer."

"You may be right, but it's time to end the playacting and go to the police," I insisted.

"I agree." Rebecca backed me up. "Tell them what you know, and let them investigate."

"I will, but I need a little more time."

"How much time?" Rebecca asked.

"A couple of days, and then I'll tell Belmont. I promise. Please don't give me away in the meantime."

"Well, all right," Rebecca agreed. "I suppose it can wait a day or two."

Janice looked relieved. "Amanda, do you agree?"

"Sorry, Janice. I can't go along. The police should be notified immediately. You're obstructing their investigation. They don't even know who the murder victim is."

"I don't see that a couple of days can make much difference."

"That's not your call. If you don't report your impersonation to Lieutenant Belmont, I will."

Chapter 26

I seethed as I walked out of the police station a couple hours later. Lieutenant Belmont had accused me of grand-standing and poking my nose in where it didn't belong. Worse yet, he hadn't believed a word of my story. He'd laughed in my face before telling me to leave the investigation to the professionals and showing me the door.

Rebecca hadn't come with me. She'd insisted that she should keep her promise to Janice, but I suspected she hadn't wanted to involve herself on an official level, although she'd been willing enough to confirm Janice's identity. I imagined she hadn't wanted to upset Greg, either. She hadn't told him what we planned to do. Given his hyper-concern that a murder had happened in Lonesome Valley, he likely wouldn't have appreciated his wife's involvement in looking into the circumstances.

I didn't blame Rebecca for her reluctance to involve herself more than she already had. In fact, I felt a bit guilty for getting her into it in the first place.

Walking away from the police station, I rounded the corner and sat on the same bench where Susan and I had commiserated right after Lieutenant Belmont had interviewed us the first time. Rebecca had dropped me off at the station, and I'd told her not to wait for me.

Remembering the long uphill walk home, I decided to call for a ride. I felt tired and frustrated. I'd left Laddie and Mona Lisa alone longer than I'd anticipated. I waited impatiently although my Uber ride showed up in less than five minutes. At this point, all I wanted to do was to go home.

Rushing to greet me at the door, my furry companions presented themselves as soon as I entered the house. Mona Lisa wrapped herself around my feet, making it difficult to navigate, while Laddie pressed himself against my legs and basked in my attention when I leaned down to pet him.

I inched my way into the kitchen, both pets at my heels, and tempted Mona Lisa with a kitty treat and Laddie with a chewy, which gave me a short reprieve, long enough to make a sandwich. As soon as Mona Lisa finished her treat, she leapt to the top of her perch and curled up for a cat nap.

Taking Laddie with me, I picked up my sandwich and a glass of iced tea and went outside to eat my lunch on the patio while Laddie wandered around the backyard, stopping occasionally to roll in the grass.

When I finished my sandwich, I called him to come so that I could brush him. His long golden coat needed to be groomed, and I felt guilty that I'd neglected this chore for the past couple of days. Laddie cooperated nicely, standing still, as I directed while I ran the wire brush through his thick fur and told him what a handsome boy he was. His tail wagged constantly, so I had to hold it still to brush it, too.

When I finished, I rewarded his patience by playing fetch with him. Finally, I called a halt. He hadn't tired of the game, but I couldn't say the same, and I needed to get some work done.

Mona Lisa didn't look up when we came in. She was still asleep. We left her to her nap and went into the studio where Laddie flopped down on the floor, panting. His grooming wasn't the only thing I'd neglected this week. I hadn't done much painting. It was time to get to work.

Although I had a good number of finished paintings, I knew working steadily, rather than sporadically, made for a better habit. Despite my procrastination gene, I'd managed to create a decent size body of work.

For what seemed like the thousandth time, I resolved to paint every day, but even as I made my resolution, I knew I wouldn't keep it. I thought about the arts and crafts fair scheduled for the weekend, and I doubted that I would get to the studio to paint Saturday, since I'd be at the fair all day.

After our startling discovery that Janice was pretending to be her sister Judith and my unsuccessful visit to the police station, I'd texted Belle to call me when she had a chance. By late afternoon, she still hadn't called back, and I began to worry.

After I put my paints in the freezer and cleaned my brushes, I walked outside since I couldn't see Belle's carport from the house. Her car was parked in its usual spot, so I rang her doorbell, but there was no answer. If Mr. Big had been home, he would have started barking as soon as he heard the doorbell chime, but everything was quiet. Although it was somewhat odd, I wasn't really too alarmed, but, just to be on the safe side, I called Dennis at the feed store.

He sounded frazzled when I called, but only because he was busy.

"I haven't been able to reach Belle by phone all afternoon, either, but don't worry. She's fine. Her cousin from Prescott came into town unexpectedly. Belle told me she was waiting for her when Belle got home from her doctor's appointment.

"They're out and about, and they took Mr. Big with them. I think Belle probably forgot her phone, and I don't have her cousin's number in mine, but it's at home. If they're not back by the time I get off work, I can give her a call."

"OK, thanks, Dennis. Sorry to bother you."

"No bother, Amanda. By the way, I've already polished off more than my fair share of your pie, and it was great."

"About time for another one, then."

"I can't wait."

As I assembled the ingredients for a pecan pie, I thought about Lieutenant Belmont's brush-off. I'd vowed never to speak to the man again, but I'd felt compelled to tell him that the murder victim hadn't been identified correctly. I might as well have saved my breath, but I knew the truth would come out eventually, and then he'd feel like a fool for ignoring me.

I didn't know whether to try to pursue the matter by informing the police chief or to let matters take their course and wait for Janice to confess her deception to Belmont in a couple of days.

After I slid the pie into the oven to bake, I decided to inform the police chief. If he reacted the same way Belmont had, I'd hit a wall, but I figured I should try. He might react differently; he might listen to me.

"Here goes," I said to myself as I called the non-emergency number for Lonesome Valley's police department. When I asked to speak to the chief, I was told he was out of town. After I declined to leave a message, I remembered that Ralph knew the chief. He'd lobbied him to re-open the Roadrunner as soon as possible after it had been designated a crime scene.

I looked up Ralph's number in the gallery's members'

directory and called him. It was after five by this time, so I knew Ralph had left the gallery, and Janice wouldn't be able to overhear any of our conversation. She'd been livid when I hadn't agreed to keep her secret, and I didn't particularly want to have another encounter with her anytime soon.

Ralph picked up my call on the first ring. He didn't even ask why I wanted the police chief's cell phone number.

"I have it written down somewhere, Amanda. Hold on."

I could hear papers rustling in the backround before he picked up the phone again.

"Here it is." He read me the number and then repeated it.

"Got it. Thank you, Ralph."

"You probably won't be able to reach him until Sunday night or Monday," he told me. "He's gone fishing with his brother. If they went to their usual spot, it's remote. He'd have to drive into the closest town to get cell phone reception. He might do that to check in with the station, but he left Lieutenant Belmont in charge, so he may not."

Although I didn't have much hope of reaching the chief, I called him anyway. He didn't answer, so I left a message that I needed to speak to him about an urgent matter.

Mr. Big's singular yipping brought me back to the moment. I glanced outside and saw Belle waving good-bye to her cousin as she pulled away from the curb in a classic red Thunderbird. A few minutes later, Belle called, apologizing for missing my earlier text message. She confirmed that she'd forgotten her cell phone when she'd gone out with her cousin. She sounded tired, so I kept my story short as I filled her in on Janice's deception.

When I dropped the pecan pie off later, I stayed long enough to satisfy her curiosity about the twins, but I didn't linger. I could see that Belle was tired after her busy day.

By the time I got home, switched on the television, and watched a Victorian costume drama on Netflix, I began to wish I'd made a second pie for myself. I headed to the kitchen in search of dessert, but frozen pie crusts didn't exactly fill the bill. I had to be satisfied with cinnamon toast. Belle and Dennis weren't the only ones with a sweet tooth.

Chapter 27

Although the conundrum of Janice's impersonation continued to bother me, the day of my first studio tour had come, and I needed to concentrate on preparing for it, but before I could think about getting organized, I wanted to take Laddie for a walk. I felt a bit nervous about taking part in the tour because I'd never done it before, and the experience would be a lot different from talking to potential customers in the gallery. In my own studio, every painting would be one of my precious babies. I loved them all.

If my work wasn't to my visitors' taste, I hoped they'd leave quickly, without making any negative comments. I'd learned that many people didn't hesitate to state their blunt opinions about artwork that didn't appeal to them, and I'd never developed a thick skin when it came to criticism of my paintings. Whenever customers made negative comments about one of them, I couldn't help feeling hurt. Luckily, it didn't happen too often, or I'd be a bundle of nerves, rather than slightly uneasy at the prospect of my first open studio tour.

Since it was only six o'clock, and I knew Belle wouldn't be awake yet, Laddie and I were on our own. He'd be disappointed if we didn't go to the park, so we headed that direction, Laddie prancing energetically beside me. We saw lots of other dog walkers already in the park when we arrived. Since we didn't normally come so early, I'd had no idea it would be so busy. Every time we encountered a walker with a dog, my retriever wanted to make friends, so I stopped to chat with other pet parents several times as we circled the park.

I was on the lookout for Rebecca, but it was Greg who was walking their terriers alone.

"Rebecca's still asleep," Greg told me as the terriers and Laddie playfully jumped at each other. "She's not what you'd call a morning person. I like to get out and about early myself. How was your coffee break yesterday?"

For a minute, I drew a blank. Then I remembered Rebecca had told Greg we were meeting for coffee.

"Oh, fine. The Coffee Klatsch has great lattes," I said noncommittally. I was sure Rebecca still hadn't told Greg the real reason for our meeting.

"That's good." The little terriers had started barking, and he paused to shush them. When he told them to sit, Laddie obediently joined them in doing the same. "By the way, Amanda, I hope you're taking precautions. I heard the police released their murder suspect."

"They did, and I know Susan. She didn't do it. They really don't have any evidence against her."

"If that's the case, then the real killer's still on the loose. Just be careful, Amanda. You could be in danger. You found the body, and the killer might think you saw something, even it you don't realize it."

"I'm keeping my doors and windows locked," I assured him, "but tonight I'm on the art studio tour, so, of course, the studio door will be open for any visitors who might want to drop by."

Greg frowned. "Maybe you should cancel it."

"No way. I went through a lot just to get on the tour, and this will be my first one. It's part of my business, Greg. I can't just arbitrarily cancel."

Greg didn't look convinced.

"Anyway, I can always call my next-door neighbors for help if I need it. They're on the alert."

I didn't tell Greg that it was Chip they were on the alert for, not a murderer.

"Well, OK. You better have the police on speed dial, too."

"I'm sure everything will be fine. Maybe I'll even sell a painting."

Although I appreciated Greg's concern, I didn't think I was in any danger, but I could understand why Rebecca hadn't told him about Janice. The murder had definitely set him on edge, and it was obvious that his concern was real.

As Laddie and I walked home, my golden boy's tail never stopped wagging. He was a happy camper without a care in the world. I wished I could say the same.

After Laddie cooled down and stopped panting, I fed him and Mona Lisa and brewed a pot of Earl Grey for myself. While I sipped my tea, I made myself a to-do list for the studio tour. I wondered whether I should serve food or perhaps wine and hors d'oeuvres, as was traditional at gallery show openings.

Tour hours were scheduled for six to nine. Dennis brought his spotlight over and trained it on the sidewalk leading to the studio, even though it wasn't yet dark. A few minutes before six, he rolled the sign he'd made for me out to the curb and set it up while I assembled cheese cubes on a silver tray I'd borrowed from Belle and decanted a bottle of wine. I had another bottle chilling in the refrigerator in case I needed to replace the first bottle. I arranged some frosted sugar cookies I'd made for the occasion on a plate for folks who preferred a sweet snack.

I set out the wine, cheese, and cookies on a small table in the studio and turned on the overhead lights as well as the track lighting that illuminated the paintings displayed on the walls. I'd added a label beside each painting, like the ones we used in the gallery, with the title of the work, its dimensions, and its price. I left the easels with my works in progress in place, but I didn't plan on working on them during the tour. I was far too nervous to attempt a live demonstration of my technique.

"All set," Dennis reported. "I'm going to put the trolley in your carport until the tour ends, so it won't be in your way."

"Dennis, I can't tell you how much I appreciate your help."

"Glad to do it, Amanda. Just call if you need anything. Belle will be over later to keep you company," he said before he left.

Laddie gazed at me forlornly. I'd barred him from coming into the studio by putting a baby gate in the doorway. He was taller than the gate, and he could easily look over it. He whimpered softly as he watched me. I'd have preferred to have him with me in the studio, but my visitors might not appreciate being greeted by a dog, even a friendly one, and some people were simply scared by a big dog. I went to Laddie and petted him as he crowded the gate, but he settled down after I consoled him.

He perked up when he heard voices outside, but he didn't try to jump over the gate. A young couple entered, helped themselves to the wine and cheese, and looked around. Although I greeted them and asked them if they were looking for anything in particular, they said they were just looking and rebuffed all my attempts to engage them in conversation. They didn't seem to be in any particular hurry as they each downed their first glass of wine and poured themselves a second. I didn't offer to supply another bottle, so when the wine ran out, they left.

I stepped over the baby gate, and Laddie followed me while I went to the refrigerator for the second bottle of wine and more cheese. I gave Laddie a dog biscuit for being a good boy. My visitors had completely ignored poor Laddie while he'd watched them, wagging his tail the whole time.

The tour hadn't gotten off to the best start, but as I set out the cheese cubes and another bottle of wine, I told myself that the rude young couple hadn't behaved in a typical manner. I could only hope that the next visitors would be an improvement.

About half an hour later the next group, a woman with three young children, showed up. As soon as the kids saw the cookies, they made a beeline for them. There were two girls, about six and three I guessed, and a boy, maybe four or five. When the older girl saw Laddie, she picked up a second cookie and gave it to him. Needless to say, he enjoyed his unexpected snack, but one was more than enough for him, so when she grabbed another cookie and started for Laddie, I asked her not to. After I gently explained that too many cookies weren't good for dogs, she pouted and clung to her mother.

In the meantime, her sister had stuffed a whole cookie into her mouth and she began to choke. Her mother patted her on the back until she coughed.

"Could we have a glass of milk, please?" she asked.

"Sure," I said, leaving them alone in the studio. I poured a small glass of milk for the little girl, returned as quickly as I could, and gave it to the child. She drank about half of it before exclaiming "all done!"

"Give it to Mommy," her mother said, holding her hand out for the glass, but instead of handing it over, the little girl tossed the glass toward her mother's outstretched hand. The glass shattered on the floor, leaving a nasty puddle of milk and jagged shards.

"Be careful," I warned, with visions of a liability suit if one of the kids slipped on the spilled milk or cut themselves on the broken glass. I pulled a broom and some old towels out of the studio's supply closet and began to clean up the mess while the mother apologized.

As I checked to make sure I'd removed all the broken glass, the boy, who'd been very quiet during all the commotion took a cookie from the platter, walked over to one of my unfinished canvases, and held the cookie up to it, frosting side facing the picture.

I ran to the child, grabbed my canvas, snatching it out of his reach, and told him to stop, but I wasn't quick enough. He'd succeeded in rubbing a wide streak of frosting across the entire painting before I could reach him.

At least his mother had the grace to look embarrassed as she hustled her brood toward the door. "Sorry," she mumbled as she grabbed her son's hand and pulled him along.

"Unbelievable," I said as I stared at my injured landscape.

"What's unbelievable?"

"Belle! A friendly face at last!"

"I take it things haven't been going too well," she said looking at my painting that the little boy had attacked with his cookie.

"That would be an understatement," I said, proceeding to recount what had happened so far. "I think maybe it was a mistake to offer food and wine. It might be too much of a distraction. If I didn't have it available, people could concentrate on the artwork."

"Can you salvage your painting?"

"I'm not sure. I hope so. I should put it in the other room, out of sight, before anyone else comes."

"Don't give up yet, Amanda. It's only seven o'clock." Belle glanced around the studio. "Everything looks wonderful. Serious buyers and sincere lookers will appreciate it. It must have taken you all afternoon to arrange and label all your paintings."

"It did, but now I'm not sure it's going to be worth it," I sighed.

"Have a cookie, Amanda," Belle said, offering me the platter and helping herself to one. It'll make you feel better. Mmm, this is delicious."

I took a large bite, and my mouth was full of cookie when my next visitor arrived. Belle caught my pleading look and greeted him with a hearty "hello," giving me enough time to swallow before I said anything.

"Good evening, Mr. Miller," I said, wondering why he would attend a studio tour. The last time I'd seen him, he'd been hightailing out the front door of the Roadrunner after Ralph called the police.

"Good evening, uh . . . ." He stopped mid-sentence to consult the flyer. "Amanda. So we meet again."

I introduced Belle, but he barely took notice. He sauntered over to the table where the untouched second bottle of wine sat, picked it up, and poured himself a glass after examining the label.

"Not bad for a cheap wine," he commented after taking a sip.

"Really, Mr. Miller," Belle said, her disapproving tone unmistakable.

"Oh, don't get me wrong," he said. "I'm not objecting. It wouldn't make good business sense to serve a better wine. I serve Michelle Brut at my gallery openings, not Dom Pérignon."

Belle looked somewhat mollified while I stood there waiting for the other shoe to drop. It didn't take long.

Brooks circled the studio peering intently at each painting that hung on the walls while Belle stood next to the baby gate and petted Laddie, who regarded the newcomer with curiosity. Brooks didn't acknowledge my perky pet at all. I could picture Brooks getting out his notebook and writing a critique as he'd done in the Roadrunner.

After he'd viewed every painting on display, he turned to me and smiled.

"I wouldn't make this offer to everyone, but I'd like to invite you to exhibit your artwork in my gallery."

Horrified at the thought of displaying my paintings alongside his, I had to control myself not to make a face. "But I'm already in the Roadrunner."

"I'm aware of that, Amanda. I'm not asking you to change locations."

An uneasy feeling came over me. "What do you mean?"

"I'll be taking over the Roadrunner's location and expanding my offerings beyond my own work. I want only the best in the new gallery."

That let his own artwork out, but since he evidently had no idea how bad his paintings were, the irony escaped him.

"I thought Judith decided not to sell the building."

"She'll come around."

"She seemed quite adamant about it after you left the other day."

"Tempers flare, but good business sense will out in the end. It was a mistake to try to speak with her in person. My lawyers and real estate agent can handle the details from now on. When the Roadrunner's members learn about the scandal Judith was involved in, they won't want to have anything to do with her."

"What scandal?" Belle asked.

"Maybe I've said too much already, but I have it on good authority that the media will be breaking the story in the next few days. You'll hear about it soon enough. Trust me: when the news comes out, Judith won't want to show her face in any art gallery in the country."

He set his wine glass down.

"You really should consider my offer, Amanda. You'll be in a real gallery, not a cooperative, with professional representation. My wife will take over as gallery director, and she'll personally train the sales staff, so there'll be no amateur hour."

If I hadn't known how bad Brooks's own artwork was and the high-pressure sales tactics his wife used, I'd almost have been tempted.

"Think about it, Amanda," he urged before he left.

"He seems like a jerk," Belle said, "But his offer sounded kind of good. Am I right in assuming that if you took him up on it, you wouldn't have to work in the gallery?"

"That's right, but there are a couple of sticking points, and, of course, Brooks doesn't know that Judith's dead, and he's still dealing with Janice."

I stepped over the baby gate into my living room and invited Belle to do the same. Laddie was beside himself with joy now that there was no barrier between us. I sat on the sofa, patted the cushion next to me, and Laddie jumped up beside me, putting his head on my lap and soaking up my attention. Belle smiled as Mona Lisa joined her on the wide arm of the chair when she sat down. The calico kitty allowed Belle to pet her although my finicky cat refused to lie on Belle's lap.

"We'll be more comfortable in here. I don't know why it didn't dawn on me earlier that I don't have to stay in the studio waiting for visitors all evening. I can see cars parking in front perfectly well from right here."

"True. What was that you were saying about sticking points?"

"Oh, right. I don't think I mentioned it to you, but the day Dustin and I shopped downtown, we went into the Brooks Miller Gallery on First Street."

"If he already has a gallery here in Lonesome Valley, why does he want another one?"

"Better location, but his artwork is terrible. I mean it's really, really bad, but obviously he doesn't know that. He acts like he's Picasso reincarnated."

"So not a good thing to be invited to show in his gallery?"

"Definitely not, and there's something else. We met his wife at his gallery that same day, and she believes in high-pressure sales. She wasn't above flirting outrageously with Dustin in hopes of making a sale. She even agreed to a date with him."

"But she's married."

"Exactly. Dustin didn't know that when he asked her, though. He ended up canceling."

"Sounds like he dodged a bullet there."

Suddenly, Laddie reared up and ran to the front door. I could see an old Lincoln stopping in front of my studio tour sign.

"Looks like we have another visitor. Sorry, Laddie," I said as I stepped over the baby gate.

"I'll stay in here with him," Belle called, but Laddie stationed himself next to the gate so he could see what was going on in the studio.

A middle-aged couple entered. They declined my offer of wine, but the woman plucked a cheese cube up and popped it into her mouth. "Cute toothpicks," she commented as she discarded the red curlicued toothpick in the small trash container I'd placed next to the little serving table.

While her husband wandered around the studio, the woman looked intently at one of my partially finished paintings displayed on an easel.

"So you go from this," she said pointing to the landscape on the easel, "to that." She waved toward one of my paintings that hung on the wall.

"Yes."

She seemed interested, so I explained my process.

"I'm afraid we don't know much about art. We're new in town, and we picked up the flyers for the studio tour downtown. By the way, that's a beautiful scarf you're wearing."

"Thank you. I tie-dyed it myself."

"I love the light and dark blue colors. You don't happen to sell scarves, too, do you? I'd really like to buy one."

"I never thought about it, to tell you the truth. I make them for myself and to give as gifts once in a while, but, sure, I could make you one if you like."

After we settled on terms, the woman who introduced herself as Faye Anthony, decided she'd like to buy two scarves, one blue and one pink. When she gave me cash for a deposit, I promised to have them ready for her in a week. She planned to stop by to pick them up during the next Friday night studio tour.

The Anthonys ended up being the last visitors of the evening. Although we left the sign out until nine, nobody came during the last hour.

"At least you made a sale," Belle said.

"True. I'm sure that doesn't always happen. I tend to get overly optimistic about these events sometimes. At least the tour wasn't a total disaster."

After Dennis brought my sign back inside and removed the spotlight, we finished the wine and cheese, and then they went home. I think they would have stayed a little longer, but they saw me stifling a yawn, and Belle commented that I must be exhausted.

She was right, although my exhaustion was more mental than physical. As soon as they went home, I decided to go to bed early, but, try as I might, I couldn't fall asleep. I had so many things on my mind I felt like a juggler with three balls in the air, all about to come crashing down unless I could keep my momentum going.

Thoughts about the murder, Janice's impersonation, and Brooks's obsession with buying the Roadrunner all spun around in my head. At the same time, I couldn't help dwelling on my odd studio tour. I'd only had nine visitors, but I guessed that probably wasn't unusual, given that we opened our studios to the public weekly.

I lay awake for quite a while. Finally, I decided to get up and read. I pulled on a robe, and a sleepy Laddie followed me to the living room, but Mona Lisa stayed in bed curled up on the pillow that she'd claimed as her own.

I leafed through some art magazines I'd checked out from the library, pausing as I paged through them to read some of the articles. Snoring softly, Laddie lay at my feet. I knew he wouldn't go back to the bedroom until I did. I glanced at the clock and saw that it was close to midnight. I didn't have to be at the arts and crafts fair until nine o'clock, so I wasn't especially worried about a lack of sleep. There was still plenty of time for that. I picked up another magazine. I'd just started to read an article about an artist, now eighty, who hadn't started painting until she was sixty when I heard a noise.

It sounded like a door handle rattling, and it was coming from my studio!

Chapter 28

The rattling stopped, and I would have thought I'd had imagined it, if not for Laddie's reaction. He jumped up.

I'd removed the baby gate hours earlier, so there was no barrier to prevent him from running to the studio door.

I followed, turning on all the lights. There were vertical blinds on all the windows in the studio, and I kept them closed at night, so if anyone were lurking outside, the person couldn't see us, but he could certainly see that the lights were on, so he'd know someone was home.

Laddie returned to my side, an indication that whoever had been outside the studio door had left.

I turned the lights out, cautiously parted the blinds slightly and looked out, but I couldn't see a thing in the darkness. I was turning the studio lights back on when we heard a muffled bumping sound, followed by a louder thump.

This time, Laddie took off for the kitchen door that led to the carport.

I peeked through the curtain that obscured the little window on the top part of the door. Had I seen a shadow next to my car? I couldn't be sure.

Then my car alarm went off, and I *was* sure.

Even though I'd followed Greg's advice to keep my doors and windows locked, I was scared now. Someone was definitely out there, and I felt sure that he had tried to get into my house!

I reached into the pocket of my robe for my cell phone, but it wasn't there. I ran back to the bedroom and looked on the night stand, but it wasn't there, either. When I turned on the lamp beside my bed, Mona Lisa gave me a baleful stare, along with a loud "meow" to protest being disturbed.

Hurrying from room to room in search of my phone, I began to panic. I had no landline. I hoped Dennis and Belle would hear my car alarm and call for help, but I was afraid it was more likely that they'd investigate in person, perhaps putting themselves in danger.

As I rushed about the house searching for my phone, Laddie stayed beside me, prancing and wagging his tail, as though I'd invented some new game to play.

My search seemed to take forever, but it probably lasted less than a minute. I heard my phone ringing and finally located it between the cushions in the chair where I'd been sitting earlier, reading the art magazines. It must have slipped out of the pocket of my robe.

"Hello."

"Amanda, we heard your car alarm go off. Are you OK?" Belle asked.

"Someone's prowling around the house! I was going to call the police, but I couldn't find my cell phone until just now when you called me."

"Dennis is on his way over. I'll call the cops right now."

I found my car keys on the kitchen counter and fumbled with them, finally managing to shut off the alarm with my trembling hands. Then I turned on the carport light and watched for Dennis. He soon appeared, flashlight in hand. When I saw him coming, I opened the door to let him inside.

"Someone's been out there, all right," Dennis told me. "Your trash can's overturned, and some branches on the bush under your bedroom window are broken off."

The siren of a Lonesome Valley police cruiser wailed somewhere close by. We listened as it grew louder. Lights flashing, the police car stopped in front of my house, and the siren abruptly stopped. An officer carrying a police-issue flashlight emerged from the vehicle and strode up the front walk to my door.

Laddie ran to meet him. Everyone was his buddy as far as Laddie was concerned, and he greeted his visitor with his usual happy tail-wagging enthusiasm.

"Mike!" I exclaimed.

"Everybody OK here?" he asked, patting Laddie at the same time.

"Yes," I said, "but I heard somebody prowling around the house. It sounded like he tried the door handle to the studio, and my neighbor here said my trash can has been overturned."

"Dennis Compton, officer," my neighbor introduced himself. "My wife and I live next door, and we heard Amanda's car alarm going off. When she told my wife somebody was lurking around outside, I came over to check it out."

"You stay here, and I'll have a look around," Mike said, nearly running into Belle as he turned around.

"Sorry it took me so long to get over here," Belle said breathlessly. "I had to get dressed first."

Instinctively, I pulled my robe closer. I was about to head back to my bedroom to pull on some jeans and replace my fluffy slippers with sandals when another car pulled up behind Mike's police car.

"It's Greg," Belle said, opening the door wider and calling to him.

"What are you doing here?" she asked bluntly. "Don't tell me you went out for a midnight snack."

"Hardly. I was home monitoring the police band when I heard the call. It was in the neighborhood, so I thought I'd come over to find out what was going on. I didn't know the call was to your house, Amanda. What's going on?"

I repeated the prowler story, and Belle introduced her husband to Greg, who immediately began trying to convince Dennis to start an official neighborhood watch group for our block.

"This is the first time we've ever had any trouble around here," Dennis told Greg, "but we do watch out for each other."

Mike returned and closed the front door behind him. Five people and a large dog all clustered within a few feet of each other created a claustrophobic feel in my small living room, but Laddie was having the time of his life, making the rounds and soaking up attention from everyone.

"Amanda, do you have any idea who might have been trying to break in?" Mike asked.

"No, I don't. Except for my artwork, there's nothing valuable here, but I can't believe someone would want to pilfer my paintings."

"You did have an open studio tonight, didn't you?" Mike asked. "People could see what you have."

"I did, but how did you know about it?"

"I saw the flyer. They're all over town. Maybe someone found a picture he liked and decided to come back and help himself."

"Considering who showed up, I very much doubt that," I

said. "A couple who were more interested in drinking wine than looking at art, a young mother with three kids, and a lady who came in with her husband and bought some scarves from me."

"Don't forget Brooks," Belle added.

"Brooks? You mean Brooks Miller?" Mike asked. "The same guy who was causing trouble at the gallery?"

"Yes. That's the one."

"As rich as he is, I doubt that he'd swipe a painting."

"What about Chip . . . ? Dennis suggested. "He's been bothering Amanda."

Mike insisted on hearing all the details. Greg looked at me in surprise while Belle told Mike about the young artist's interest in me.

"Where can I find this Chip?" Mike wanted to know.

"He works at his father's pizza parlor, The Pizza Palace," I volunteered, "but I can't believe he'd do something like this. I think he's just a harmless flirt."

"We'll see about that. What's his full name?"

"Travis Baxter."

"You don't happen to know where he lives, do you?"

"No idea."

"I'll track him down. In the meantime, I'll maintain patrols in the neighborhood to keep an eye on things. Call 9-1-1 again if there's any trouble."

After Mike left, Greg insisted on having a look around the yard, so Dennis accompanied him, although he wasn't enthused about Greg's constant urging to form an official neighborhood watch group on our block. In Dennis's opinion, he was already on the alert and didn't need to formalize it.

Belle invited me to spend the rest of the night at her house, but I declined. If I was going to get any sleep at all, it would have to be in my own bed. I never could sleep the first night in a strange bed; it always took me a while to get used to a different mattress.

Greg and Dennis returned, and Greg reported that they'd checked all the doors and windows to confirm that they were still locked up tight. We thanked Greg for his concern, and he left reluctantly after I turned down his offer to stay in his car out front to keep an eye on my house.

Although Laddie fell asleep right away after we went back to bed and Mona Lisa didn't budge from her nest on the pillow, I tossed and turned the rest of the night and woke groggy and out of sorts when Mona Lisa pounced on me and began tapping my arm with her paw. At least, she was polite about it and didn't scratch me.

After I tended to Laddie and Mona Lisa, I revived a little after taking a long shower and brewing a pot of strong black tea.

Belle had invited Laddie to stay with her and Mr. Big while I helped staff the Roadrunner's booth at the arts and crafts fair, so we left Mona Lisa to her own devices. As we went out of the house, my calico kitty bestowed one of her mysterious smiles on us. If I hadn't known better, I would have thought she held the secrets of the universe in her Mona-Lisa smile.

Chapter 29

Susan had texted me she was on her way and given me directions to the Roadrunner's white tent, located close to the park's pavilion. After walking around for a couple of minutes, I spotted it. I'd arrived early to find Chip and Lonnie setting up the grids where our members' artwork would be displayed.

"Thanks a bunch, Amanda," Chip said sarcastically when he saw me.

"What are you talking about, Chip?"

"I had a little visit from the police last night. It seems they suspected me of trying to break into your house." Shifting gears to his puppy-dog, hurt voice he continued, "Why would you suggest to them that I'd prowl around your house in the middle of the night? You know me better than that."

I didn't actually know him at all, I thought.

"I didn't say anything, Chip. My neighbor told the officer you'd stopped by the house before, and it sounds like the police took it from there."

"Good thing I had an air-tight alibi then. I was helping Dad clean up after we closed last night."

"I'm sorry they paid you a call."

Chip looked at me closely. I knew I had dark circles under

PAULA DARNELL

my eyes, and although I'd tried to cover them with make-up, they were still visible. "No, I'm sorry, Amanda. You look as though you didn't sleep at all last night. You must have been terrified."

"It was a little scary," I admitted.

"Hey, Chip, let's get a move on," Lonnie called. "The members will start coming to hang their paintings any time now, and I need to get going. I have to babysit while Heather gets her hair done."

"Sorry, Lonnie," Chip muttered. He made quick work of finishing the grids' set-up. After they finished, Chip said, "You go ahead. I'll take care of the rest."

Lonnie didn't object, and he took off in a hurry while Chip upended the folded six-foot table we'd be using to display our prints and note cards, pulled the legs out, pushed them to lock them in place, and set the table upright.

"Just in time," Chip said. "Here comes Aunt Susan."

Susan pulled two large rolling suitcases behind her. She stooped to unzip one of them and pulled out a dark blue table drape. I helped her position it over the table. It extended all the way to the ground and fit perfectly. That was handy because we could hide the suitcases under the table where nobody could see them.

"I can tell you've done this before," I said, as Susan began pulling display props out of her bags.

"Oh, yes. Many times. Chip, I left the prints and note cards in my trunk. Do you have time to get them?"

"All the time in the world for you, Auntie," he said with a grin.

"And don't call me 'Auntie,'" she scolded good-naturedly, tossing him her car keys.

Chip winked playfully at her as he walked off, whistling.

Susan sighed. "Honestly, I don't think that boy will ever take anything seriously."

After that comment, Susan and I didn't really have a chance to chat because members began arriving with their paintings, and Susan started to place them on the grids. I'd forgotten to bring mine to our booth, so I had to return to my car to pick them up.

I'd chosen two small realistic portraits I'd painted about a year earlier. They weren't in my usual expressionistic style. Instead of my typical landscapes, I'd painted appealing pictures of my pets, which I'd originally intended to hang in my family room in our home in Kansas City. They never went up on the wall after Ned revealed he planned to divorce me. I decided that, if either painting sold, I could easily make another to keep for myself.

"How adorable!" Susan said when she placed the portraits of Laddie and Mona Lisa side by side on the grid. "They're so lifelike. I didn't know you painted pet portraits, too."

"Just for myself and to give as gifts, usually."

More members arrived with their paintings, and I noticed that although most of them greeted Susan and interacted with her as they normally would, a few snubbed her. By the time Susan had placed all the paintings on the grids in an attractive display and I'd set up the boxes of prints and displays of note cards on our draped table, Susan was teary-eyed.

"Just ignore those people, Susan," I advised her.

"I've known most of our members for several years. It's hard to take; that's all. Do they really think I'm a murderer?"

"Come on, Aunt Susan. Amanda's right. Don't pay any attention to them. They'll come around, and if they don't, they're not worth knowing, anyway."

Susan pulled a tissue from her jacket pocket and dabbed her eyes. "Thank you for believing in me, both of you."

A few customers had begun to arrive, but the fair was hardly crowded yet.

"Why don't you and Amanda go look at some of the other booths while I stay here to man our space? It'll take your mind off those jerks."

"Ok, sure," Susan agreed, and I nodded my assent. "I'd like to look around a bit, but call us if it starts to get busy."

Most of the sellers offered craft items, although there were a few artists in attendance. We passed booths featuring wooden birdhouses, yard signs, candles, soaps, and wreaths, before encountering a familiar face. The high school student I'd spoken with when her class visited the gallery was busily arranging a necklace on a bust while her mother was setting out business cards and brochures.

"Oh, hi," the student greeted me. "You're the lady from the art gallery."

"You have a beautiful display," I told her. "Are all your beads and pendants handmade?"

Both mother and daughter enthusiastically began explaining how they made their ceramic beads and pendants. It was fun to listen to them finishing each others' sentences. They were definitely on the same wavelength, and their obvious closeness touched my heart and made me long to see my own daughter. I'd have to be patient, though, and wait until her summer break at college before I'd have the chance to spend some time with Emma.

"I'd like to buy this one," Susan said, pointing to a necklace that featured a large iridescent blue-green ceramic dragonfly. I don't need a bag. I'm going to wear it right now."

Susan paid cash for her purchase, and the student removed the price tag and handed her the necklace along with a receipt. I bought a pair of beaded earrings and a brooch shaped like a bear. I pinned the brooch to my scarf and tucked the earrings away in my purse before we moved on.

We hadn't gone far before Susan's cell phone buzzed.

"We need to get back," she told me. "Chip says a crowd has gathered."

We hurried back to the Roadrunner's tent. Chip was processing a transaction on our mobile credit card device, and there were two customers waiting in line to pay for prints they'd selected.

"Excuse me," a woman wearing a bright red maxi dress said. "Could you tell me about the artist who painted this golden retriever?"

While Susan rushed to the table to help Chip, I turned to the woman.

"I sure can. You're speaking to her."

"Oh, great! Is he your dog?"

"Yes, he's my golden boy."

"I'm guessing the calico cat is yours, too. She looks like she's kind of smiling but not quite."

"That's why I named her Mona Lisa."

For an instant, the woman looked confused, but then she said, "I get it now. She has a Mona-Lisa smile."

"Exactly."

"I was wondering whether you ever do commission work. I'd love to have a portrait of Buster. He's my springer spaniel."

Although I'd painted only one commissioned piece in my life and never one of a pet, I felt confident in telling her that I did, indeed, accept commissions. She didn't register any shock when I quoted her the price, so I took that as a good sign. When we exchanged business cards, I saw that she was a local real estate agent.

"My schedule is flexible," she told me when I asked her if I could meet Buster in person. That would help give me an idea of his personality, which I hoped to portray in my painting of him.

"Great. We can set up a time next week, and I'll also take several photos of him for reference. You're welcome to text or email me pictures of him that you have, too."

She said she'd be in touch and insisted on giving me a hefty deposit to "reserve our spot," before she moved on to the next booth.

"She didn't buy anything?" Susan asked. "She seemed so interested."

"She did, actually," I told Susan about my new commission, and she squealed with excitement.

"That's wonderful, Amanda! All Chip and I have sold are some note cards and a few prints."

"Bravo, Amanda," Chip said. I noticed he'd dialed his flirtatious ways back, whether because he was still a bit peeved at having to provide an alibi to the police or because his aunt was present.

Now that I'd seen the mural he'd painted for Janice and learned that she considered Chip her protégé, I'd been wondering whether he recognized the woman pretending to be Judith as his mentor, but it was obvious from the way he was talking about the gallery with Susan that he didn't know she was Janice, not Judith.

A few more lookers drifted into the booth, and I answered

their questions about the paintings on display, but they didn't buy anything. Susan advised me not to spend too much time with the "tire kickers," as she called them, but, unlike the high school student who sold jewelry with her mom, I still hadn't developed the ability to discern when a potential customer was serious. Maybe that skill would come after I'd worked in the gallery longer and hosted more studio tours. I hoped so, anyway.

Around noon, we took turns visiting the food vendors for lunch. By the time the Lonesome Valley Pioneers gathered on the pavilion's risers for their performance, we hadn't sold a single painting, only several prints and note cards. Customers were interested in the lower-priced items; they hadn't come to the fair to buy pricey art, but their buying preferences came as no surprise since Susan had warned me that most of the shoppers would be looking for craft items.

A crowd began gathering in front of the pavilion where benches had been placed for people to sit while they watched the singers. To see the performance, all I had to do was step outside our tent, since we were close by. The singers, all dressed in Western garb, filed in and took their places, kicking off their program with "America, the Beautiful." After the crowd applauded enthusiastically, Rebecca stepped forward to sing the first verse of the next number.

> *You got to visit Lonesome Valley.*
> *You got to see it for yourself.*
> *Bring somebody else to visit with you.*
> *Don't got to see it by yourself.*

The altered lyrics of the mournful old tune turned it into something of a Chamber of Commerce advertisement for Lonesome Valley and its attractions as the song continued with three more verses, each sung by a different choir member, and then wrapped up with a repetition of the first verse, sung by the entire choir.

"That's a new one," Susan commented. "I've never heard them sing that before. I guess it's meant for the tourists."

She'd joined me outside the tent. We had no customers at all. Now that the program had started, everyone who'd been in the vicinity had taken a seat on one of the benches to listen to the choir.

The Western-themed show continued with familiar tunes such as "Red River Valley," "Don't Fence Me In," Home on the Range," and "Oh, Shenandoah." After several more numbers, Greg came to the front. I'd been surprised earlier to see that he was part of the choir because Rebecca hadn't mentioned it when she'd told me she was a member. I noticed that Greg looked a lot more rested than I did, despite his midnight foray to my house.

Greg's rousing rendition of "Ghost Riders in the Sky" rivaled Johnny Cash's version, sending a chill up my spine, and was followed by a thunderous round of applause from the audience. The singers all bowed, and each soloist came to the front to take a bow. Greg was last, and the clapping increased when he took his final bow.

As the crowd dispersed, I managed to catch Rebecca's eye and wave to her. She grabbed Greg's hand, and they threaded their way through the people who drifted back towards the booths.

"Wonderful performance!" I greeted them. "Congratulations!"

I introduced them to Susan who had watched the entire show with me. I knew Greg recognized her name because, as soon as I said it, he lifted his eyebrows. I was glad he didn't mention her arrest. Susan and Rebecca chatted about the choir's costumes for a few minutes before Susan returned to the tent to help a customer.

"I didn't realize you sang, too, Greg," I said.

"Oh, sure. Rebecca and I were in the choir together in high school."

"Really? High school sweethearts, then?"

"Not quite," Rebecca said. "Greg was a couple of years ahead of me, and we hung around with different crowds. We didn't start dating until we were both in college."

"You must have known Janice and Judith in high school," I said to Greg.

"I knew who they were. It's a small high school, but, like Rebecca said, they were all younger."

He looked past me into the Roadrunner's booth.

"That looks like Laddie," he said, pointing to my painting.

"It is."

"I'm going to take a closer look," he said, leaving Rebecca and me alone.

"Have you heard anything yet?" Rebecca whispered. "Janice should be going to the police today."

"So she said, but I'm not sure she'll do it. Since Lieutenant Belmont refused to believe me, I tried to contact the chief of police, but he hasn't called me back. I understand he's out of town for the weekend."

"Well, something has to give. I can't keep the news from Greg much longer, and I'd rather he hear all about it from Channel 2 than from me. He seems to suspect something's up. He keeps asking me about our coffee date, and he freaked out when he heard the police call last night. He's convinced you're in danger, and he could be right. Promise me you'll be careful, Amanda."

Greg was heading our way, so I just nodded.

"That's some great picture, Amanda," he said. "I don't know how you do it."

"And I don't know how you two do it, either—singing the way you do. I can't even carry a tune."

We all laughed.

"Take care of yourself, Amanda," Greg said, echoing his wife, when Chip called me back to the booth. "And don't forget to keep your house locked up tight, whether you're home or not."

"I won't forget." I assured him. His hyper-vigilance could get a little much sometimes, but he had a point, so I didn't ignore him. If I'd forgotten to lock the door to the studio last night, the prowler could have walked right in, and who knew what would have happened. I shuddered to think about it.

Chapter 30

We enjoyed a steady, but small, stream of lookers, so Susan and I decided to take turns seeing the rest of the fair. We hadn't gotten very far before Chip had called us to return to the Roadrunner's booth in the morning.

"Let me know if it gets busy," I told Susan as I left. "I won't be long."

"Take your time," she suggested. "We can handle it."

I wandered off in the direction of the food vendors. My lack of sleep was catching up with me, and I couldn't wait to drink a strong cup of coffee. I didn't like to carry a drink into any vendors' booths. Even if I had a cap secure on the cup, an accident could happen. I remembered all too well the little boy who'd decided he wanted to improve my painting with a streak of cookie frosting.

Of course, I had no such intention, but a bumped arm or a careless movement could easily result in an accident that could ruin a vendor's item, so I sat at a picnic table near the food booths and drank my coffee there. When I finished, I pitched my paper cup into a large trash can.

"Hi, Amanda."

For a split second, I didn't recognize him without his uniform.

"Oh, hi, Mike. Off duty, I see."

"Yep. By the way, we questioned Travis Baxter, and he isn't the one who tried to break into your studio."

"I know. We're both working at our Roadrunner booth today. Chip told me the police had paid him a visit. He wasn't too happy about it."

"We had to check, but he was our only lead. The door handle and window sill had been wiped clean, so there were no fingerprints."

"I didn't realize you'd checked for fingerprints."

"Yep. Sorry we couldn't come up with anything. Take care, Amanda. Don't hesitate to call if you need help."

"Don't worry; I won't. Thanks, Mike."

I walked down the nearest aisle, enjoying the warm, sunny day and the vendors' displays. I stopped to buy some cute decorated treats for Laddie and Mona Lisa at a pet bakery's stall. They looked like cookies, which appealed to pet parents, although the treats certainly wouldn't taste like them. I hoped finicky Mona Lisa would take to her snack, and I had no doubt that Laddie would love his. He'd never been a picky eater.

I tucked the plastic bags of treats into my purse and continued browsing, but I didn't stop until I came to a booth filled with small sculptures of animals. From a distance, I couldn't tell what the artist had used to make her sculptures, so I entered the tent to take a closer look.

"They're all made of wool," a white-haired lady who looked to be in her mid-seventies explained. "I use wool roving and sculpt them by needle felting. Whenever I need a certain color, I hand dye the roving."

"They're marvelous," I said. "You ought to join the Roadrunner Gallery and sell them there." Too late, I remembered that Pamela had told me an artist who worked with wool roving had been turned down for membership. One glance at the woman's face confirmed my fear that she was that artist. Now, I'd really put my foot in it.

"I'm so sorry; I didn't mean to upset you," I apologized.

"There's no way you could know, but I applied for membership, and they turned me down. That gallery director—that Janice woman—acted as though I had no right to apply for membership. Then she gave me the brush-off when I tried to talk to her about it. My grandson tried to intervene on my behalf, but she wouldn't talk to him, either. I know she's a murder victim and all, but I can't say I'll miss her. She wasn't a very nice woman."

I was about to say that she should re-apply, but I thought better of making that suggestion since Janice was indeed alive and would undoubtedly continue as gallery director. Instead, I turned the conversation back to her artwork, and she gave me a quick demonstration of her technique.

"I admit I didn't know what needle felting entailed before you showed me," I told her. "It's amazing the way you shape the wool using just a needle. It must take a long time."

"Yes, it's quite time consuming, but I enjoy it. This is the first time I've displayed my critters at a show, but I've sold several of them already."

I noticed that her prices were quite low, considering her artistry and time spent on each sculpture, but she seemed happy with her sales, so I hesitated to suggest that she raise her prices.

She stared past me and waved. "Here comes my grandson," she said proudly. "He went to get me some iced tea."

I turned around to look at him and was surprised to see a familiar face.

It was Mike.

Mike Dyson was her grandson.

"Here you go, Grandma," Mike said, handing her a cup.

He nodded at me. "We meet again."

"I never could have set up my booth today if Mike hadn't helped me. I had no idea how to put up a tent."

She glanced at him proudly, and he blushed at her praise.

"You know I'm always happy to help, Grandma."

"So that's why you're here at the fair—to help your grandmother. I thought your family lived in Phoenix."

"All except Grandma," he said, looking at her fondly.

"There's too much hustle and bustle in the big city for me. I like Lonesome Valley just fine, but I'm afraid it's a little too sleepy for Mikey."

"It's like they roll the sidewalks up at sundown. Lonesome Valley's not a bad place, but there's not much going on."

It seemed to me there was quite a bit going on, including an unsolved murder, but I understood what he meant. For a young man his age, the local attractions probably weren't nearly as exciting as a trendy nightclub or a Suns' basketball game.

"I'd better get back to our booth, so my friend has a chance to look around," I said. "I'm glad you're having a good day today. Best of luck tomorrow."

As I walked back toward our booth, I realized that Mike had a motive for the murder, and since he was the first responder to arrive, if there was any evidence on or around the body, he could have easily removed it. Even though Susan and I had both been there, too, we were so shocked and upset that we probably wouldn't have noticed a thing.

I tried to tell myself that my imagination was running wild, but all the pieces of the puzzle fit.

It was entirely possible that Mike had murdered Judith.

Chapter 31

Not that I thought he'd planned it. It seemed much more likely that his temper had flared when Judith denied knowing anything about his grandmother's rejection. Maybe he'd flung the bronze bear at her in the heat of the moment. Stunned, perhaps she'd stumbled into the hallway where she collapsed.

He'd been on patrol in the downtown area that morning, and Judith, seeing a uniformed officer at the gallery door, must have let him in herself.

I didn't want to believe it of Mike. He seemed like such a nice young man, and he'd always been perfectly polite to me, but I couldn't get away from the facts that not only did he have the means to commit the murder, but he'd also been in a perfect position to have the opportunity. It had never dawned on me that he might have a motive, too, until I found out about his grandmother's rejected application to the Roadrunner.

I couldn't share my suspicions with Lieutenant Belmont. He hadn't believed me when I'd told him who the real murder victim was, but I felt I should tell somebody—somebody who could act on the information. I'd have to wait until the chief of police contacted me to tell my story. I only hoped he wouldn't react the same way Lieutenant Belmont had with his don't-be-silly sneer.

PAULA DARNELL

Back at the Roadrunner's booth, a few browsers were looking over our paintings, but they soon moved on, and Susan took the opportunity to look around the fair for herself, leaving Chip and me in charge. When she'd asked me to help, she'd told me that Chip and Lonnie would set up our tent, grids, and table in the morning, but she hadn't told me Chip planned to spend the day. Without Susan as a buffer between us, this could be awkward.

"Why don't you sit down for a while, Amanda? You look tired." Chip repositioned a plastic lawn chair behind the table, pulling it back so that it didn't look as though I were the cashier.

"All right," I said, happy to be off my feet for a while. I'd been standing all day, and my lack of sleep the previous night wasn't helping my alertness.

"Even though you look tired, you still look cute."

"Oh, please," I groaned. "Don't you ever give up, Chip?"

"I mean it, Amanda. You're a very attractive woman."

I wasn't in the mood to engage in repartee with him, but I was saved by the bell when his cell phone rang. He pulled it out of his pocket, looked at the display, and walked away from our tent, out of earshot. Pamela was probably calling him, I guessed, and he didn't want me to hear their conversation.

After about ten minutes, Chip returned to the booth.

"That was Pamela," he said, "and she has bad news."

"Is she all right?" She'd had to leave the gallery in a hurry when her housekeeper called her to tell her about a flooding problem at her house, and I hadn't seen or heard from her since.

"She's fine, but we're going to have to do something about Judith."

"What do you mean?"

"She's in big trouble. Evidently, she was selling forged art in her Texican Gallery, and not just a few pieces, either. Supposedly, she actually hired some artists to create the forgeries, but the new owners found out, and now they're suing her for fraud. It's not only civil charges, but criminal that she'll have to deal with. Pamela told me that a warrant was issued for her arrest in Texas yesterday. Most likely, the local cops will be asked to pick her up, and she'll be extradited back to Texas unless she turns herself in first. There goes our gallery director and maybe our only chance to keep our rent-free space for the Roadrunner. She'll probably have to sell the building to pay for her legal fees."

So Brooks had been right, I thought.

"I wouldn't be too sure about that," I said. This bit of news would finally elicit the truth from Janice about her impersonation of Judith. She might be in some hot water for withholding evidence, but that paled in comparison to the trouble she'd be in otherwise. If she kept trying to pass herself off as Judith, she could easily end up in prison, and Judith's fortune was bound to be depleted if the new owners of her former art gallery prevailed in their lawsuit against her or her estate, when they learned she had died.

Chip looked confused. "You mean you think she's innocent?"

"No. I don't know whether she is or not. All I'm saying is that it's best to take a wait-and-see attitude. Let things play out and take it from there."

"You just said a lot without saying anything. Do you know something you're not telling me?" He looked at me closely. "You do."

I never did have a poker face.

"What is it, Amanda?"

"I can't tell you yet, but suffice it to say that things should sort themselves out in the next few days."

"You're being very mysterious."

"Let's wait to see what happens. That's really all we can do, anyway."

"Pamela wants to have a board meeting tomorrow afternoon to explore our options."

"I guess it couldn't hurt." By the time they held the board meeting, Janice's deception could well have been exposed.

Chip's phone rang again. He took the call right away, not bothering to step outside the tent.

"OK, Dad. I'll be there in ten minutes," he said a few seconds after answering. "I have to go in to work right away," he told me. "One of our drivers is having car trouble, so I need to cover for him. Are you OK here alone?"

"No problem. You go ahead. Susan will be back soon, anyway."

Chip rushed off, and, as luck would have it, a crowd gathered in our booth as soon as he disappeared. I was busy processing a sale for one of Ralph's paintings when Susan came back and pitched in.

"That's as busy as we've been all day," I said as soon as the rush ended.

"We've taken in quite a bit of money," Susan said. "Even though most of our customers charged their purchases, the man who bought Ralph's painting paid cash, and it was the most expensive item we had on display. We have over seven hundred dollars here, and I don't feel comfortable taking that much money home."

"Would you like me to drop it off at the gallery before

closing? They can include it in the night deposit."

"If you don't mind, that would be great, but you'd better get going. The gallery will be closing soon."

We quickly assembled our copies of the day's receipts and the cash we'd accumulated. I was a bit nervous about carrying that much money around, but I knew some people routinely carried hundreds of dollars in cash in their wallets. Ned was one of them. He'd done it for years without problems.

"I'll close up here," Susan said. "The organizers of the fair hired security guards to patrol tonight, so we're going to leave everything in place. Thanks so much for filling in, Amanda. I know it was a long day for you, especially after the prowler incident at your house last night. We're covered for tomorrow, so get some rest."

"It was a fun day, but I plan on it."

I tucked our cash envelope and folder with our receipts into my handbag and scurried off with a wave to Susan. I couldn't wait to get home to relax and hang out with my pets, but I'd volunteered to drop off our proceeds from today's sales because the gallery was on my way home, but not on Susan's. As I walked to the parking lot, I pulled my phone out of my pocket to call Belle, but it rang before I had the chance to make my call.

"Amanda, it's Susan. Pamela just called me, and a few of the gallery members want to get together a little later, after the fair closes. Evidently, there's some problem with Judith that Pamela wants to talk about before the board meeting tomorrow, but she wouldn't give me any details. We're going to meet at Pamela's studio. Can you come?"

"I don't know, Susan," I said wearily. "I'm awfully tired, but I'll try to make it. I can't promise, though."

As soon as Susan rang off, I called Belle. At the same time, a text from Pamela showed up on my phone, inviting me to come to her studio for a buffet dinner and informal get-together, but I didn't answer right away. I wanted to talk to Belle first.

"Hi, Amanda, how was the fair?" Belle asked.

"Fun, but I'm tired. How are Laddie and Mona Lisa doing?"

"Just fine. Laddie's happy to play with Mr. Big, and Mona Lisa came down from her perch when I went over to your house to check on her. She played with her toy mouse for a while, and she ate the kitty treats I gave her."

"I've been invited to Pamela's for dinner. I think it's really more of a meeting about the gallery, but I'm not sure I should go. I don't want to put you out. You and Dennis probably have plans for the evening."

"We do. Here's our plan: stay home and fire up the barbecue. Don't worry about Laddie or Mona Lisa. I can give them dinner. Relax and stay as long as you like."

"Thanks, Belle. I'm still not sure I'm up to it. I'm just so tired. I don't know. I can't decide."

"Either way, we'll be right here, so take your time."

I was still undecided when I said good-bye to my obliging friend. I answered Pamela's text, telling her I wasn't sure about coming, but I'd be there if I perked up a bit.

I arrived at the gallery a few minutes before closing time. Ralph was behind the counter, and Janice was talking with a small group of tourists.

"Ralph, you'll be happy to know that one of your paintings sold at the fair," I said. "In fact, it was the only original artwork we sold all day."

"Which one was it?"

"Your smaller picture of the mountains in moonlight."

"Great! I'll bring another one around in the morning to replace it, but you didn't need to come by to tell me about it."

"Actually Susan wanted us to include our cash sales with the gallery's night deposit. I brought the cash, and here are the sales receipts." I placed them next to the cash register and counted the cash into stacks of hundreds while Ralph watched.

"Sure. We can do that. I'll start the reconciliation, and then Judith can verify my count before I take it to the bank."

"In the meantime, would you mind if I print a few inventory sheets here? I'm planning on changing my wall display here tomorrow, but my printer's out of ink."

"Sure. Help yourself," he said motioning toward the computer. "There's some kind of a problem with this printer here, so select the remote printer, and it'll send your documents to the printer in Judith's office. You can pick them up there. Looks like she's still tied up with those tourists, so use the spare key. He produced a small key with a shoelace attached to it from beneath the counter and handed it to me.

"OK, thanks, Ralph," I said, wrapping the shoelace around my wrist before clicking the form on the gallery's website. After I hit the remote print button, I went down the hallway to the office to retrieve my inventory sheets.

I unlocked the office and plucked the papers from the printer. When I glanced at them, I could see that the top sheet wasn't one of mine. I took a closer look.

It was a boarding pass in the name of Judith Warren—a boarding pass for a flight from Sky Harbor Airport in Phoenix to São Paulo, Brazil, via Mexico City and Santiago, Chile. The flight's departure time was only a few hours away.

Janice was getting ready to fly the coop!

Chapter 32

My first thought was that, like Pamela, Janice had heard that a warrant had been issued for Judith's arrest, and she'd decided to continue her impersonation despite it, so she was fleeing to Brazil where there was no extradition treaty with the United States.

But that didn't make any sense.

Why play the part of her sister when it meant leaving the country to escape prosecution?

Then it hit me.

Janice was going to Brazil to avoid the law, so that *she* wouldn't be charged.

Janice had killed her own twin!

I was sure of it.

Only a few hours earlier, I'd felt certain that Mike was the culprit. Now, I knew better, but I didn't have time to dwell on the guilt I felt about suspecting an innocent man.

"What are *you* doing in here?"

I'd left the door to the office open. When I turned, Janice was standing in the doorway, and she didn't look happy.

"Just printing some inventory sheets. Ralph told me that the printer up front was jammed, so he said I should use this one."

Like a naughty schoolchild caught doing something wrong by the principal, I felt obliged to justify my actions.

"I see," Janice said, grabbing the papers out of my hand as she strode to her desk. It happened so fast I didn't have time to protest. She glanced down and saw the boarding pass immediately.

"So you know."

"Know what?" I said, although it was difficult to feign ignorance at this point.

"You know I'm leaving for Brazil tonight."

"I think there's a little more to it than that."

From the way Janice's face contorted with anger, I knew I'd made a mistake as soon as those words were out of my mouth.

"Ralph!" I yelled as loudly as I could.

"Ralph's left for the day, so you may as well save your breath," Janice said. "We're all alone."

She pulled out the top drawer of her desk and whipped out her gun, pointing it straight at me.

Feeling light-headed, I wobbled a bit and had to steady myself by bracing my hands on Janice's desktop to keep from falling over.

"Sit down, Amanda," she commanded, motioning to a sturdy wooden chair with wide arms next to the side of her desk. "You're becoming a real nuisance."

"You're not going to—?" My words hung in the air.

"Shoot you?" Janice finished my thought. "Only if you make me. If you cooperate, you'll spend an uncomfortable night, but Valerie will find you when she opens the gallery in the morning, so you might as well save your breath. Do we understand each other?"

Despite my fear, her I'm-the-principal tone irritated me. I didn't answer.

"I said 'do we understand each other.'" She raised her voice this time.

"No, as a matter of fact, I don't understand you at all, Janice. You had a perfectly nice life here and a good position as gallery director. You're a top-notch sculptor. Why would you throw all that away?"

"I didn't mean to do it. Judith always could get under my skin. This is her boarding pass, you know," she said, waving it in the air. "She showed up, saying she wanted to reconcile and spend some time with me, but it was all about getting her ducks in a row before she left for South America. We got into one of our shouting matches, and she turned her back on me. I know she did it deliberately. I never could stand that. I told her to turn around and face me, but she just kept on walking."

"So that's when you clobbered her with your bronze bear," I guessed.

"My bear? Of course not! I'd never do anything to damage one of my own sculptures. I threw my gun at her. I was trying to make a point. I wasn't trying to hit her, but my aim was off. I put the bear on the floor as a distraction to throw the police off. I figured it would take a while for the cops to discover it wasn't the murder weapon."

"But why impersonate Judith?"

"Because she was in a lot of trouble, and it was all going to come out soon. Nobody would wonder why she fled to Brazil. All I had to do was keep up the charade until it was time to leave, but you and Judith's snoopy friend had to stick your noses in where they don't belong."

"That's why you wanted to stall when I asked you to go to the police to tell them Judith was the victim, not you."

"By the way, thank you for not reporting my impersonation.

I was sure you were going to."

"I did report it."

"I don't believe you. The cops would have picked me up by now."

I shrugged. "It could happen any time." I wasn't about to tell her that Lieutenant Belmont hadn't believed me, and was, in fact, not planning on questioning her.

Then something else occurred to me.

"Did you try to break into my house last night?"

"I don't know what you're talking about." She truly seemed at a loss.

"Put your arms on the arms of the chair," she directed as she pulled the shoelace with the key to the office dangling from it off my wrist. I had no choice but to comply; she still had the gun trained on me.

After I moved my arms, she rummaged around in her desk with her left hand. She pulled out a ball of twine and pulled the end of the cord. Holding it in her teeth and keeping the ball of twine in her left hand and the gun pointed at me, she managed to wrap twine around my right wrist several times until I couldn't wiggle it. She repeated the same maneuver with my left wrist.

Then she placed the gun on the desktop, several feet away, although I couldn't have reached it anyway. She proceeded to tie a series of intricate knots in the twine, first on my right wrist, then on my left. I struggled to pull free, but she kept tightening the knots.

"Ouch!" I cried. "You're cutting off my circulation."

"You'll be fine," she said, without sympathy, "and so will I. I'm setting up a new studio in São Paulo, now that the last of Judith's assets have been transferred to her bank account there.

I'll miss the Roadrunner, but I'm guessing its members won't miss me. I'll practice my Portuguese on the flight there. Tchau."

Chapter 33

With that, she yanked the landline cord from the wall and smashed the phone on the floor. Then she grabbed her gun, along with her boarding pass, and flipped off the light switch before closing the office door firmly. I heard the key twisting in the lock, followed by a scraping noise. I was sure she'd propped a chair under the door handle to make it harder for me, should I try to escape.

In the small, windowless room, I felt like I was in a prison cell. The darkness only added to my panic, which I was trying to check by telling myself that, even if I had to wait until the gallery opened in the morning, I'd survive. Somehow, that thought did little to calm me, though.

At least there was something I could do about the darkness. I stood at best I could, or rather leaned over with a heavy wooden chair on my back, and staggered toward the door. The sturdy chair didn't make the task easy. I knew the light switch was right next to the door, and when I got that far, I sat back in the chair, slipped off my right sandal, raised my leg, and tapped around on the door with my toe until I felt the light switch and pushed it up. Now that I could see what I was doing, I felt determined to try my best to escape.

If only I had my cell phone with me, I might be able to make an emergency call by poking it with my toe or maybe my nose, since I had 9-1-1 on speed dial, but I'd put it in my purse after I'd counted out the cash for the gallery's night deposit and given Ralph the receipts from the fair. Intending to be gone only a minute to pick up my inventory sheets, I'd left my purse beneath the counter next to the cash register.

Ralph hadn't heard me call him, so he must have gone to the bank right away, leaving me alone with Janice. He'd have no reason to be concerned about that at all. Nobody, except Janice, knew where I was, and I wouldn't be missed for quite a while. I'd told both Susan and Pamela that I wasn't sure I'd join them for the gathering at Pamela's studio, so they wouldn't think anything about it when I didn't show up, especially since I'd mentioned to both of them how tired I felt.

My only hope was Belle, who would realize something was wrong when I didn't come home. Unfortunately, she'd told me to take my time, so she wouldn't start worrying for hours yet. Right now, she and Dennis would be enjoying a barbecue on their patio while the dogs romped in the backyard. Tears trickled down my face as I thought of the peaceful scene, but dwelling on it wasn't helping me get out of my predicament.

By this time, my panic had subsided a bit, and determination began to take hold. The twine Janice had wrapped around my wrists felt terribly tight. I didn't think I could stand it if I had to wait until morning to be rescued. My only hope was to try to undo the knots Janice had tied in the twine.

It was a good thing Janice hadn't gagged me, or I wouldn't be able to use my teeth to do it. She must have figured that she needed only enough time to drive to Sky Harbor in Phoenix and board her flight. Once the plane took off, she'd be on her way to Brazil. Granted, there were a couple stops along the way, but, logistically, it would probably be hard to stop her once she left the United States.

Resolutely, I bent over my right arm and crunched my incisors between the twine of the first knot, trying to loosen it. It gave only slightly. I crunched and pulled for several minutes with my teeth before I succeeded in undoing the first knot, but I felt encouraged that I might be able to undo all of them eventually.

An hour later, I'd finally come to the last knot. Frustrated, I'd stopped and resumed my biting and pulling motions several times, but now that I could see the end in sight, I pressed on.

After I unraveled the last knot, I had to flip the twine off my wrist and around the arm of the chair. Finally, I raised my wrist and yanked it free. Ugly, deep red welts covered my wrist, and my right hand felt numb. I made a fist and released it several times in an attempt to restore better circulation.

Now that my right arm was free, it wouldn't be nearly as hard to free my left arm. Bouncing the chair up and down, I bumped my way across the floor so that I could reach the drawers of Janice's desk.

I pulled the top center drawer open, the same one where she'd kept her gun, and I found I was in luck. Lying neatly in an organizer tray was a pair of scissors with pointed ends. I grabbed them with my right hand and began hacking at the twine that still bound my left wrist. Unfortunately, the scissors weren't especially sharp, so it took several minutes to cut through all the twine. The second I did, I let loose a whoop. Finally, my arms were free!

Of course, I was still locked in the office, but at least I could move around. I stood up and walked back and forth in the small room, rubbing my wrists. The left one looked even worse than the right one. The rough twine would have been irritating enough against delicate skin, but since Janice had wrapped it so tightly, my wrists still hurt, even though I'd removed the twine.

I turned the doorknob on the off-chance that Janice hadn't properly locked the door. Of course, she had, and I'd heard her propping a chair under it in any case. If I wanted to get out of the office, I'd have to break the knob and dislodge the chair.

I examined the door and saw that there was enough of a gap at the bottom to slide a yardstick underneath it. I grabbed the metal measuring stick that Janice kept propped up in the corner behind her desk. Then I lay on the floor in front of the door and slid the yardstick under it. I began poking it this way and that until I connected with one of the chair's legs. Then I pushed it steadily, until I heard the chair clatter to the floor.

That obstacle removed, I looked around for something to batter the door handle with. Although Janice kept a bronze wolf on her desktop, I bypassed it and looked for something else. I couldn't quite bring myself to use a piece of artwork so roughly, but I knew I'd need a heavy object to break the door handle, and nothing else in sight fit the bill.

Desperately, I yanked open the other desk drawers. I found a small metal toolbox in the bottom drawer. I upended it on the top of the desk to empty its contents, but after hitting the doorknob with the little metal box a few times, I could tell that it wasn't heavy enough to do the job.

I examined the knob more closely and could have kicked myself for not noticing that the knob's screws were on the side of the door facing me, not on the outside. All I had to do was remove the screws and dissassemble the knob, and I had just the right tool to do it. Among the items I'd dumped onto Janice's desktop, I found a Phillips screwdriver. I was in business. It took me only a couple of minutes to remove the screws, take off the door handle on my side and reach through the opening to thrust the outer handle off the door. I pushed the door open and went into the hallway.

I felt tired and hurt and desperate to use the restroom, but I was free.

Chapter 34

I ran down the hallway to search for the light switch. When I entered the gallery, I heard pounding on the gallery door, and I could see the beam of a flashlight moving back and forth in the dark. As soon as I flipped on the light switch, I ran to the door. For a split second, I imagined that Janice had returned to the gallery, but the thought disappeared almost as soon as it came to mind. In the highly unlikely event that Janice had returned, she would have let herself in with her key.

"Mike! Am I ever glad to see you!" I said, as I opened the gallery door.

He took one look at my swollen wrists, marked with unsightly red welts, and asked me what had happened.

"I was kidnapped; that's what happened. Janice threatened me with her gun and tied me to a chair in her office. Then she locked me in." My words tumbled out quickly.

"Whoa! Slow down, Amanda. Let's take it one step at a time. You said Janice locked you in, but Janice is dead, remember?" He looked at me with concern.

"I'm not hallucinating, Mike; I promise you. Janice is very much alive. Her twin sister Judith was the one who was murdered. Janice killed her own sister, and she's been impersonating her ever since."

Mike shook his head in confusion.

"Didn't you come here looking for me? I thought maybe my neighbors alerted the police when I didn't come home."

"No, I came here to take Judith Warren into custody because she's wanted in Texas." He frowned. "Show me where you were locked up."

I was afraid that Mike didn't believe a word I'd told him, and time was running out, but maybe if he saw the scene of my imprisonment, he'd take me more seriously. I led him down the hallway so he could see the scene for himself. The chair Janice had propped under the doorknob lay on its side, and the metal parts of the knob were strewn about, while two lengths of the twine Janice had used to tie me up were still lying on the office floor, along with parts of the doorknob.

Mike emitted a long, low whistle.

"Look, Mike, Janice is on her way to the airport in Phoenix, and she's booked on a flight to Brazil. She's using Judith's name. If somebody doesn't stop her before she gets on that plane, it'll be too late," I said urgently.

"OK, Amanda. All this business about switching identities is above my pay grade. The higher-ups will have to sort that out, but we can alert the Phoenix police to pick her up before she boards the flight. The warrant's for Judith Warren, and you say she's booked under Judith's name. You don't happen to know which airline or the flight number, do you?"

I closed my eyes and tried to picture the boarding pass. "I'm sorry, Mike. All I remember is that she goes through Mexico City and Santiago, if that helps. And the flight leaves soon."

"I'll call it in. Maybe the Phoenix police can apprehend her."

He used his cell phone, rather than his radio, to call the

station, and he didn't mention a word about Janice's impersonation of her sister, although he reported that I'd been held at gunpoint and tied up.

"Let's go on down to the station, Amanda," he said after he finished the call. "You can give all the details to Sergeant Martinez."

"What about Lieutenant Belmont?"

Mike shrugged. "I don't know. He hasn't been in all day."

I retrieved my purse from under the counter and turned out the lights. Mike made sure the gallery door locked after he pulled it closed on our way out.

When he opened the door of his police cruiser for me, I asked if I could follow him in my own car.

"I don't think that's a good idea, Amanda. You're shaking like a leaf."

So I was, but I hadn't realized it until he told me. As I looked down at my trembling arms, a car screeched to a halt in back of the police car, and Dennis jumped out.

"Are you all right, Amanda?" he yelled.

"Yes. Could you let Belle know? I have to go to the police station to file a report."

"I'll do better than that. I'll go get Belle, and we'll meet you there."

When Mike and I arrived at the station, we saw a woman going in ahead of us carrying a pizza box. She gave it to Sergeant Martinez, along with a kiss, and I recognized her as Dawn, the gallery member who had a ceramics studio with her mother Dorothy Weber. I remembered that Dawn's last name was Martinez. I hadn't made the connection before, but now I realized the sergeant must be her husband.

Dawn took one look at me and insisted I sit down while she

went to find a first-aid kit. She carefully applied antiseptic to the raw skin on my wrists while I related my story to her husband.

He looked doubtful when I told him that Janice was pretending to be Judith, but Dawn saved the day when she commented that she'd thought something was odd about Judith.

"So Janice has been there the whole time," Dawn said. "I thought Judith acted just like Janice, but everybody I mentioned it to passed her behavior off as normal for a twin."

"She admitted to me that she killed her sister. She said she threw her gun at Judith and hit her on the head. She claims she didn't mean to hit her."

"I don't know about that," Dawn said. "Janice has a mean streak."

"That'll be for the jury to decide," her husband said. "Lieutenant Belmont's going to have egg all over his face on this one," he muttered as the station door opened.

Belle and Dennis burst in, but they weren't alone. Laddie and Mr. Big had come with them. Belle, Laddie, Mr. Big, and I came together for a group hug, and Laddie stuck to my side like glue as I told my incredible story for the third time.

Meanwhile, Sergeant Martinez alerted the Phoenix police that a fugitive was about to leave the country.

Sergeant Martinez didn't object to our canine companions' invasion of the police station, but, after an hour or so, he did tell me I might as well go home, although I should be available the next day to sign an official statement and speak to Lieutenant Belmont or the chief, if he came back from his fishing trip early.

"What about Janice?" I asked. "Will the Phoenix police let

you know whether they were able to stop her?"

"I'll see what I can find out," Sergeant Martinez said, as he picked up the phone.

After a brief conversation, punctuated by "yes," "right," and "good" on Sergeant Martinez's end, he gave us a thumbs-up sign.

"They took her off the flight just as the last boarding call was announced. She's in custody now."

"She almost got away with it," I said.

"She came close," Sergeant Martinez agreed.

"I think it's time to go home now, Amanda," Belle suggested.

"I think you're right."

Laddie and I piled into the back seat of Belle's car, and Mr. Big hopped in behind us. The dogs seemed happy to have some extra excitement in their lives.

"Let's pick up your car tomorrow, Amanda," Dennis said.

"Sounds good to me," I leaned back and closed my eyes while I petted Laddie with my right hand and Mr. Big with my left. I couldn't wait to get home.

As Dennis was about to pull into his driveway, a bizarre scene unfolded on the sidewalk in front of my house.

A man held both hands in the air while another man stood behind him.

"That's Greg," Belle cried as Dennis stopped the car. "But I don't recognize the other guy."

I leaned forward. Now that they'd moved under the street lamp, I could see them more clearly.

"I do," I said. "That's my ex-husband."

We all jumped out of the car, and Laddie ran to Ned, but when he didn't lower his arms, Laddie returned to my side.

"What's going on, Greg?" Dennis asked.

"After last night's incident, I thought I'd drive by and check Amanda's house. I found this joker poking around."

"I was not," Ned protested. "I was waiting for Amanda to come home."

"You can put the gun away, Greg. This is Ned, my ex-husband, although I have no idea what he's doing here."

"OK, fella," Greg said reluctantly. "This isn't a gun, anyway." He held up a hard plastic tubular container. "I thought it might feel like one without the cap on it. It's the bottle for my high blood pressure meds. Fooled you, though," he told Ned.

Ned looked disgusted that he'd been taken in by Greg's ruse.

"Were you here last night?" I asked Ned point blank.

Ned shifted uncomfortably. "I thought I might drop by to surprise you."

"In the middle of the night? You scared me half to death."

"Sorry, Amanda. Uh, could I talk to you alone for a minute?"

"Say what you have to say, Ned. It's late, and I'm tired. My friends can hear whatever you have to say."

Belle, Dennis, and Greg stood their ground.

"I think I've made a mistake. I was hoping we could talk about getting back together."

I almost laughed in his face. "Go home, Ned. Go back to your wife and your baby. I have a new life here, and I don't want to go back to my old one."

"But you can't possibly be happy here," Ned said, "in a tiny house a quarter of the size you're used to."

"You're wrong, Ned. I *am* happy here."

Despite my financial problems, my struggle to get my new art business off the ground, and having been locked in Janice's office tied to a chair, I realized it was true.

Chapter 35

As it turned out, Ned's unexpected visit wasn't the only reminder of my old life in Kansas City that weekend. When I checked my email late Sunday afternoon, I found a message from a Kansas City resident who'd attended the party given by the judge and his wife. She'd seen the commissioned painting I'd made for them and wanted to inquire whether I had time in my schedule to paint a scene of her backyard for her. She'd attached several photos showing blossoming fruit trees and mentioning that she loved my expressionistic style. I didn't waste any time responding to her query, and by the end of the week, we had a contract signed.

I also paid a visit to the real estate agent I'd met at the arts and crafts fair. Buster, her English springer spaniel, greeted me at the door, wiggling with excitement at having a visitor. After spending some time with him, I couldn't wait to capture the personality of the playful, energetic dog on canvas. Although painting his beautiful brown-and-white coat and soulful eyes required technical skill, bringing out his personality in a portrait meant going a step beyond, but that extra step was the difference between a mundane picture and a fascinating portrait, and I had every intention of painting a fascinating portrait of the lively spaniel.

With two commissioned paintings in the works, my financial situation was looking up. I resolved to stick to a stricter, more regimented work schedule than I'd had since I'd moved to Lonesome Valley.

A smaller boost to my income came when the woman who'd ordered two tie-dyed scarves from me told her friends where she'd ordered them. After I received a few more scarf orders, I decided to make several to display and sell during my Friday night studio tours. Although a scarf sale netted a fraction of the price of a painting, those sales added up, and I soon found that I almost always sold a few scarves during the studio tours, but I seldom sold a painting then.

Although my art business fared well in the weeks following Janice's arrest, there was one part of it that remained up in the air—the Roadrunner Gallery. Even though Janice was confined in the county jail, awaiting trial, she still wanted to control the gallery, but it soon became clear that she'd have to sell it to pay her attorney.

Of course, I shared all the latest news of the gallery with Belle. She'd first heard about the roller-coaster ride with my gallery membership the day of my interview when I'd been sure my membership application would be rejected, and we'd brainstormed ideas about what I should do.

* * *

"Mmm, I love this pie," Belle said, as we sat at my little table on a sunny morning in May, enjoying the apricot cream pie I'd made the night before.

"Warm up?" I asked as I picked up the coffee pot.

"Yes, thanks. So what's the scoop? You said you had some news."

"Hot off the presses. Susan called me a little while ago. You know that Janice has been negotiating a sale of the Roadrunner's building with both Brooks and Pamela."

"You told me she was pitting one against the other, trying to get an exorbitant price."

"That's right, and I'm afraid Pamela had just about come to the end of her rope. Her husband agreed it would be a good investment, but he never wanted to pay a price that would be substantially over market value."

"So Brooks wins?"

"That's just it. He doesn't. Janice really doesn't want Brooks to put his own gallery in the Roadrunner space. From what Susan tells me, Janice is appalled at the prospect, so she's decided not to sell the building, after all."

"But I thought she needed the money to pay her legal fees."

"She told Chip she's going to agree to the plea deal the district attorney offered her to save the expense of a trial. According to what Chip told Susan, Janice will have just enough to pay her lawyer for the work she's already done. She wants to continue to donate the space for the Roadrunner."

"I'm surprised she decided to take a plea. Remember how she kept proclaiming her innocence after her arrest?"

"Who could forget? She accused me of fabricating the whole kidnapping incident, but nobody believed her, not even Lieutenant Belmont."

"Who's going to manage the gallery," Belle asked, "now that Janice is headed to state prison?"

"I guess she wanted Chip to do it, but he turned her down. He says he has no management skills and isn't interested, anyway. Even though he won't be managing the gallery, he's still going to live there. Janice offered Chip the use of her apartment, rent-free, while she's in prison."

"That's quite a perk."

"Chip's the only person I know who really likes Janice. He's visited her several times at the county jail, according to Susan. Maybe Janice is hoping that Chip will get inspired to do more mural painting if he's living every day with the scene he painted on Janice's living room wall. It's really quite something to see."

"So who's going to be minding the store?"

"Ralph's filling in temporarily, but he doesn't want to do it long-term, so the members will have to vote on Janice's replacement. I have a feeling Pamela will probably be elected; I think she'd be a good choice."

"She's the one who helped get your studio on the tour, isn't she?"

I nodded.

"More pie?"

"I'm tempted, but I'd better pass," Belle replied, just as the doorbell's chime brought Laddie to his feet.

I opened the front door to find my mail carrier on the porch. When she'd first met Laddie, she'd been a bit wary of his enthusiastic greeting, but they'd since made friends, and she leaned over to pet him, before handing me a priority mail envelope and asking me to sign for it.

Curious, I quickly scribbled my name, and she handed over the envelope. As I closed the door, I glanced at it and saw the sender's name.

"How odd. It's from Ned. I wonder what he's up to now."

"Only one way to find out," my practical friend said.

"Here goes." I pulled the tab and yanked off the cardboard strip to open the envelope. I reached inside and pulled out a piece of paper, which was folded in thirds. I shook it, and another paper fell to the floor.

"Looks like a check," Belle said.

I stooped to pick it up, turned it over, and gasped.

"I don't believe it. Look at this." I handed the check to Belle.

"Wow! I've never seen so many zeroes on a check before. What's the scoop?"

"I wish I knew." I picked up the folded paper, but there was no note. There wasn't a notation on the bottom of the check, either.

Something Dustin had mentioned when I'd told him I hadn't received anything for my half of our family home in Kansas City was nagging me. At the time, I'd felt uncomfortable discussing our financial arrangements, and I'd quickly changed the subject.

"That doesn't sound right," I said out loud, remembering his words.

"Hmm?"

"Oh, something Dustin said when he was visiting me and I told him his father had pretty much claimed to be broke when we divorced."

"Looks like maybe he wasn't so broke, after all. Could be he's feeling guilty now."

"Maybe." I suspected that the large check I'd just received had been motivated by something other than Ned's innate generosity and that Dustin had had a hand in it somehow. I doubted that he'd ever admit it to me, though.

No matter how it had happened, I certainly planned to put my unexpected windfall to good use.

"What are you going to do with the money, Amanda?"

I didn't have to think twice.

"I'm going to buy this house."

I'd been lucky to find a house to lease when I'd moved to

Lonesome Valley, but renting had always seemed less of a commitment to my new life and my new business than buying a house.

Belle beamed, and Laddie jumped up and down in excitement while Mona Lisa crept up and pounced on my feet with an approving meow.

I smiled as I reached down to pet my furry companions. "Looks like they agree: there's no place like home."

Recipes

Baked Artichoke-Potato Frittata

Most of the time, cooks start their frittatas by heating them on a burner and finishing them in the oven or under the broiler. This recipe, the same one Dennis used to make a breakfast frittata with plenty left over so that Belle and Amanda enjoyed it for lunch, too, doesn't require the constant monitoring that stovetop cooking does since it bakes in the oven.

Ingredients

8 large eggs
¼ cup heavy cream
1 cup artichoke hearts
½ teaspoon salt
½ teaspoon coarse ground pepper
one small baked potato
½ cup onions
¼ cup sun-dried tomatoes

Directions

Preheat oven to 350 degrees.

Beat eggs, cream, salt and pepper. Do not overbeat the egg mixture. Set aside.

Use either canned or frozen artichoke hearts. Cut the artichoke hearts into small pieces. If canned artichoke hearts are used, make sure to drain them well and dry them on paper towels. If frozen artichoke hearts are used, they should be thawed and cooked. Peel the baked potato and cut it into small pieces. Mince the onion and sun-dried tomatoes into very small pieces. Combine the potato, artichoke, onion, and sun-dried tomatoes.

Butter a 9-inch by 9-inch baking dish. Place the vegetables evenly into the baking dish and then pour the egg mixture over them.

Bake approximately 25 to 30 minutes. To check whether the frittata is done, make a small slit in the center with a sharp knife. If the eggs are runny, continue baking for a few minutes. If the eggs are set, remove the frittata from the oven. Do not overbake. Let set for five minutes before cutting.

Makes six servings.

Three-Ingredient Guacamole

Amanda has learned that guacamole is all about the avocados. Use nice, ripe avocados, and no matter what extra ingredients you add to this basic avocado recipe, you'll be on the right track. Many people add garlic, onion, peppers, tomatoes, or other ingredients, but you can't go wrong with this three-ingredient recipe as long as you start with good, ripe avocados.

Ingredients

2 ripe avocados
1 lime
½ teaspoon fine sea salt

Cut the avocados vertically, from the stem to the bottom, all the way around the avocado. Remove the pits and discard them.

Scoop out the flesh with a spoon, but avoid scraping it against the shell. Discard the shells.

Mash the avocados with a fork. The avocados will be somewhat lumpy. If you prefer your guacamole to have a smoother texture, you can use a food processor.

Juice the lime and add the lime juice and the salt to the mashed avocado. Combine well.

That's it! You're ready to serve your guacamole.

If you don't plan to serve it right away, cover the surface with plastic wrap and store in the refrigerator for up to two days.

Great with tortilla chips, on sandwiches, and served lots of other ways, too. Use your imagination!

Makes six to eight servings.

Taco Casserole

Amanda garnished leftover taco casserole with some fresh corn chips so that the top would be nice and crunchy. Since taco casserole is a meal in itself, all she had to do was add some of her homemade guacamole, some grape tomatoes, and shredded lettuce. Corn chips, grape tomatoes, and sour cream all make good accompaniments, too.

Ingredients

restaurant-style corn chips
1 pound ground beef
½ medium sweet Vidalia onion
1 one-ounce package dry taco seasoning
1 eleven-ounce can niblets corn
½ cup black beans
1 cup sour cream
1 eight-ounce package shredded Mexican-style cheese blend

Garnish

shredded lettuce
grape tomatoes

Pre-heat oven to 325 degrees. Lightly grease 9-inch by 9-inch baking dish.

Mince the onion. Brown the ground beef and onion, and drain off the fat. Sprinkle with taco seasoning and mix.

Drain the corn. Add the corn, beans, and sour cream and mix.

Cover the bottom of the baking pan with corn chips. Layer half the hamburger mixture over the chips. Sprinkle half the cheese over the top. Cover with corn chips. Place the rest of the hamburger mixture on top, distributing evenly, and sprinkle with the rest of the cheese. Add crushed corn chips as the top layer.

Bake 45 minutes. Let sit for 5 to 10 minutes before serving.

Garnish with shredded lettuce and grape tomatoes. Serve with corn chips, sour cream, salsa, and guacamole.

Taco casserole is best right out of the oven. If you want to save some of the casserole for leftovers, refrigerate for up to two days. Add more crushed corn chips to the top after reheating so that the top will be crunchy.

Makes six to eight servings.

Apricot Cream Pie

Amanda served Belle this refreshing, no-bake, refrigerator pie on a warm May day. Amanda's secret to making short and easy work of whipping the cream for this or any recipe containing heavy whipping cream is to chill the cream, mixing bowl, and beaters in the freezer for half an hour before whipping the cream.

Pie Crust Ingredients

50 vanilla wafers, crushed
¼ cup butter, melted
1 teaspoon cinnamon

Filling & Topping Ingredients

1 eight-ounce package cream cheese
¾ cup powdered sugar
1 eight-ounce package dried apricots
1 four-ounce container apricot/mixed fruit baby food
1 teaspoon vanilla extract
1 cup heavy whipping cream
1 fifteen-ounce can apricot halves in juice
1 cup granulated sugar

Place the dried apricots in a container and pour the apricot juice from the canned apricots over the apricots so that they are covered with juice. Reserve the canned apricots to use for the topping. If there isn't enough juice to cover the dried apricots, add water until they are covered. Seal container and refrigerate overnight. To speed the process so that you don't have to wait until the next day to make the pie, place dried apricots in a pan, covered with juice (with enough water added to cover them, if necessary) and heat on medium low until the apricots are rehydrated.

To make the crust, crush the vanilla wafers into fine crumbs, add melted butter and cinnamon, and mix well. Press into the bottom and up the sides of an eight-inch pie pan. Alternatively, use a prepared cookie or graham cracker crust instead of making your own.

Put a mixing bowl and the beaters of the electric mixer and the heavy whipping cream in the freezer for half an hour.

Soften the cream cheese. Once it's softened, add two tablespoons of the apricot baby food, powdered sugar, and vanilla and mix well with an electric mixer until smooth. Drain the apricots, reserving the juice. Pat the apricots dry on paper towels and cut into quarters. Stir the quartered apricots into the cream cheese mixture.

Remove the mixing bowl, beaters, and heavy whipping cream from the freezer. Beat one cup of the whipping cream so that it forms stiff peaks.

Fold the whipped cream into the cream cheese/apricot mixture. Pour the mixture into the pie shell. Refrigerate for at least one hour before serving.

To make the topping, add the remainder of the apricot baby food to the reserved apricot juice. Measure one-half cup of juice and put it in a pan. Add one cup of granulated sugar. Boil about five minutes or until the sugar is dissolved. Cool.

Before serving the pie, top it with one of the canned apricots on each slice and pour the topping over the pie. Cut and serve.

Makes eight servings.

ABOUT THE AUTHOR

Award-winning author Paula Darnell is a former college instructor who has a Bachelor of Arts degree in English from the University of Iowa and a Master of Arts degree in English with a Writing Emphasis from the University of Nevada, Reno. *Artistic License to Kill* is the first book in her Fine Art Mystery series. She's also the author of the DIY Diva Mystery series and *The Six-Week Solution*, a historical mystery set in Nevada. She resides in Las Vegas with her husband Gary and their Pyrador Rocky.

VISIT HER WEBSITE
pauladarnellauthor.com

CPSIA information can be obtained
at www.ICGtesting.com
Printed in the USA
BVHW071152140221
600085BV00027B/355